JEDI QUEST

BY JUDE WATSON

THE FALSE PEACE

SCHOLASTIC INC.

New York   Toronto   London   Auckland   Sydney
Mexico City   New Delhi   Hong Kong   Buenos Aires

D0311340

www.starwars.com
www.scholastic.com

ISBN 0-439-33925-1

Cover art by Alicia Buelow and David Mattingly

12 11 10 9 8 7 6 5 4 3 2 1   4 5 6 7 8 9/0

Printed in the U.S.A.
First printing, July 2004

He had chased after one man for years. He had found him. He had fought him. He had lost him and found him again. Each time, he had vowed that this encounter would be their last.

This time was no different. Obi-Wan Kenobi wanted a showdown with Granta Omega. Once and for all, he wanted to put a stop to a criminal he knew was dedicated to bringing down the Jedi Order. Deep in his heart, he knew the showdown was near.

But he also suspected that, like the others, it would not come in a manner of his own choosing.

Obi-Wan strode through the busy streets of the capital city of Falleen, Anakin Skywalker by his side. Siri Tachi and her apprentice, Ferus Olin, were only a step behind. They had landed on the planet only the day before. Obi-Wan was grateful to his friend Siri. She had pledged to help him bring Omega to justice, and so far she had traveled halfway around the galaxy, fought an army, and worn a dress in order to do it.

Now he felt responsible for her impatience. Siri believed that problems were solved by vivid action. If there was one thing she avoided, it was uncertainty.

Obi-Wan wasn't crazy about it, either. They couldn't pinpoint Omega's location. Instead, they had to randomly search for clues to his whereabouts. They knew he was on Falleen. But they did not know where, or why.

He wished he did not have the feeling that Omega was always one step ahead. He wished that in his mind, the same scenario did not constantly revolve: He would burst into an empty room just in time to see a transport take off. Omega would have escaped again.

Obi-Wan glanced at his apprentice. He knew Anakin had no such doubts. Anakin did not consider the possibility of failure. He was not haunted by his defeats.

Other things haunted his Padawan. Things too deep for Anakin to share at one time.

Yet they worked so perfectly together now. Thoughts and feelings were shared, sometimes without speaking. There were times when Obi-Wan thought that the shadow he sensed within Anakin was gone. That the struggle to accept his role as the Chosen One had been conquered. That Anakin was at ease with where he was, and the gifts that had been given him. Obi-Wan hoped that was the case. Anakin had shared his feelings with his Master — and the release had changed him.

The Jedi moved carefully through the streets, staying in the middle of the crowds. They were dressed as space travelers, and they were careful not to attract attention. The walkways of the city were filled with beings from many worlds. The city was built on three levels, and every café, hostel, and multi-residence was packed.

Factories on Falleen were booming, and more were being built every day. In a quick survey, the Jedi had learned that most of the factories manufactured weapons. Jobs and opportunities were plentiful. Visitors from star systems all over the galaxy flocked to the small planet to make their fortunes.

But if the booming capital city made it easy for the Jedi to hide, it also made it easy for Granta Omega to conceal his activities. They had learned on the planet Romin that Omega was in league with the criminal scientist Jenna Zan Arbor. She had developed a secret drug, called the Zone of Self-Containment, which could make beings feel blissfully, if dangerously, content, leading them to forget their cares, or any need for taking action. They knew that she had not yet learned how to transmit the Zone to more than a few individuals at a time. Anakin himself had been under its influence for a short while.

The two criminals, along with the former dictator of Romin, Roy Teda, had plans to pull off a major criminal operation. The Jedi suspected they planned to use the Zone to do it. Zan Arbor had enlisted the help of a criminal gang, the Slams, to help them.

The Jedi knew that much. But that wasn't enough.

They had followed Zan Arbor and Teda here, but Omega had managed to hide them well. So far they had kept a low profile and traveled through the streets and cafés, attempting to pick up some word about the criminals' whereabouts. There was plenty of talk swirling about the best factories to work in, and who was hiring. Obi-Wan had contacted the Jedi Temple with the names of various corporations that owned factories on Falleen, but it would take some time before they could discover if any had ties to Omega. Weapons merchants often hid ownership of companies behind other companies, so that it was hard to trace who exactly owned what.

Which is exactly what Omega counts on, Obi-Wan thought.

"I've never seen this much security on a peaceful

planet," Anakin remarked, adjusting his hood as he walked.

It was true. Surveillance droids were everywhere. "They aren't all official security droids," Obi-Wan observed. He had studied the various droids over the past few hours, cataloging them in his mind. "As a matter of fact, most of them seem to be private droids. And they're armed."

"Omega?" Siri asked. Her blue eyes were keen. "Looking for us, perhaps."

"Just as we are looking for him," Ferus Olin said. "So we're even."

"Any ideas, Master?" Anakin asked him in a low tone. They had been walking through the streets for some time.

"That new factory we've heard of — Blackwater Systems," Obi-Wan said. "Let's head there. It was built quickly and already has a bad reputation among the Falleens. There are rumors that bribes were paid to the government to keep away inspectors."

The factories were built just beyond the outskirts of the city. The Jedi hopped aboard a cloud bus to take them, blending in with the other passengers. They exited at the last stop.

Here the three grand pedestrian levels were narrow and squashed together, one on top of the other, so that a tall species would have trouble on the lower ones. Large factory complexes were built on ground level and rose into the sky. They knew that at night the factories belched their toxins into the sky. The Falleens called this area the Yellow District because a constant haze of that color hung in the sky.

The Jedi were now alone here on upper walkway, underneath the yellow sky. This was not an area anyone would stroll in, and it was in the middle of a factory shift, so the workers were inside. The Blackwater Factory was at the end of the long line, more than two kilometers from the last cloud-bus stop. It was colder here. The wind howled off the vast plains outside the city and carried a special bite, tasting of the vast ice sheets from the distant mountains.

The Blackwater Factory rose in their vision as they approached. It was windowless and completely fashioned from black durasteel and stone. One main building hulked on the site, with a wing flung out from one side like a useless arm.

As he drew his cloak around him, Obi-Wan suddenly tensed. He saw one surveillance droid zoom into his line of vision. Another followed. These did not seem to be moving aimlessly. The Force surged to warn him.

"We're being tracked," he said to the others. "Move normally. Could be routine."

"Up ahead," Siri remarked, casually swinging her arms as she walked.

Ahead, a narrow alley led diagonally off the main walkway, running along the side of the main building. As they passed they darted inside and began to run. The droids would have to double back, and those few seconds could make a difference. The Jedi turned a corner, then another. They could sense rather than see that the droids were still in pursuit, but hadn't been able to get a fix on them. The alley was narrow and twisted around, connecting the factory to various smaller out-buildings.

"What now?" Ferus asked. His voice was steady, even though he was running hard. Siri's Padawan did not have Anakin's great Force connection, but he made up for it with excellent physical training and a keen mind.

Anakin's head cocked. "I hear something. This way."

Following Anakin now, they ran through the maze. They passed gravsleds and durasteel bins marked as waste. They didn't see any tiny creatures or birds here. No living thing would linger in this place if it didn't have to.

Their race ended at a tall stone wall. Anakin stopped. Now the others could hear what he had de-tected so many twists and turns before. A crowd was on the other side of the wall.

The Jedi activated their cable launchers. Quickly they scaled the wall. The crowd was just ahead, focusing on a female Falleen who was speaking. Her voice rolled over the crowd.

They jumped down and quickly moved into the crowd for concealment. The two teams had doubled back during their run and were now standing outside the main gate of the factory. The Falleen female stood, hanging on to the gate with one hand to keep herself above the crowd while she spoke into a voice amplifier headset. She was tall for the species, with the distinctive gray-green color to her scales.

". . . and we ask them, what are the wastes you produce, and what is your disposal system? And they tell us —"

"NOTHING," the crowd shouted.

"And we ask them, what is the nature of the experiments you are conducting in your secret wing? And they tell us —"

"NOTHING!"

"And we ask them, what about the four workers over the past three months who have died without any reports being filed? And they tell us —"

"NOTHING!"

"And we ask them, when you have your products

and your profits, what will you do for the citizens of Fall-een? And we know the answer, don't we?"

"NOTHING!" The crowd screamed the word.

"And will we do nothing, or will we demand what is our right to demand — a full accounting of what is made here?" the female Falleen shouted. "If our leaders will not make them obey our laws, we must! Are you with me?"

"YES!" the crowd shouted.

"Are you willing?"

"YES!"

"Are you ready to go in and find what we need?"

"YES!"

"Then come on!"

A small explosive charge went off. The Falleen female leaped to the ground. At first Obi-Wan thought she'd been hurt, but then it was obvious that she or one of her cohorts had set it off, for the gates swung open. With a cry, the crowd surged forward.

"We shouldn't be in the middle of this," Ferus said.

Anakin looked fascinated.

It didn't matter if they should be there; they were caught. The crowd was ahead of them and behind them now. As it moved, they moved with it. And then ahead, Obi-Wan saw black objects fly out from the factory.

"Attack droids," he shouted. "Take cover!"

The crowd panicked and moved backward like one great breaking wave. Then they turned and ran, back toward the walkways. The Jedi fought their way through the crowd, moving against them, toward the droids.

Obi-Wan watched the Falleen female. As soon as the droids had come, she had dropped from the gate. Instead of fleeing with the others, she ran along the outside of the gate. He knew she was heading toward the alleys. He saw her make a turn. In that direction, she would run straight into a wall.

Two of the droids peeled off and followed her.

"Anakin!" Obi-Wan called. "Let's go."

CHAPTER TWO

Anakin had seen the same thing as his Master, and he read Obi-Wan's intention before it was fully formed. They needed to talk to the Falleen. Anakin looked around quickly. There was no one in sight, and no danger of blowing their cover.

He charged toward the droids, leaping and slashing, his lightsaber moving so fast that it was back in his belt before he hit the ground. The two droids lay in smoking ruin.

Grinning, Obi-Wan kept pace with him. "Nice work."

"Don't mention it."

Siri and Ferus joined them. Racing now, the four Jedi turned a corner and saw the female Falleen futilely trying to scale the wall. She whirled and tensed when she heard their footsteps.

"We're not with Blackwater," Obi-Wan said quickly. "We were in the crowd."

She nodded. "I'm afraid we're trapped."

"The droids tracking you crashed into each other," Siri told her. "They're destroyed."

"There will be others," the Falleen said. "The factory owners have my vitals. They can track me. If I were you, I wouldn't stick with me. I'm afraid my back is literally to the wall."

Anakin admired her bravery. She spoke coolly, but he could feel that inside she was terrified.

"The wall," Obi-Wan said, "is not a problem."

He strode forward and attached one end of his cable launcher to the Falleen's utility belt. "Always be prepared," he said. His tone was light, and Anakin knew he was trying to reassure her.

The Jedi moved forward. In a few seconds, they had activated their launchers and swung up and over the wall, Obi-Wan keeping the Falleen steady as they climbed. They dropped down on the other side.

The Falleen looked around. "I know a back way to the cloud-bus stop from here," she said. "I'm Mazara, by the way."

She gazed at them curiously.

"We arrived on Falleen recently," Siri said. "Looking for jobs."

"We'd better hurry," Obi-Wan said. "It won't take them long to look further."

Mazara took them on a different path through the maze of alleys that ran behind the factories. They had to scale the locked gates between the properties, but they saw no new evidence of tracking droids.

Mazara waved at the surrounding plains as she walked. "This is why Falleen is so ideal for them," she told them. "There is plenty of land outside our city. Transports can land and take off without being logged in. Waste can be dumped or offloaded onto orbiting platforms." Her voice was full of disgust. "Not to mention that as Falleen, we don't like to raise our voices. The population is growing distressed with the situation, but no one says anything. It is not 'appropriate,'" she said, giving a wry twist to the word. "Believe me, I'm not an activist. I was a journalist, before I got fired for writing an article on Blackwater. Both our land and our skies are becoming dumping grounds. I've seen it happen to other worlds. I can't watch it happen to my homeworld."

"Why did you target Blackwater Systems?" Obi-Wan asked.

"They are the worst offenders," Mazara answered. "The factory was built quickly, with little regard for basic safety practices. Enormous bribes were paid to inspectors to overlook violations that are part of the laws of Falleen. There have been several deaths at the facility and each time an investigation is done the result is the same — the worker was at fault."

"Do you know who the owners are?"

Mazara sighed. "It is the usual game of company behind company. But this muddle seems murkier than most. I've been investigating almost since they arrived, and I don't have any answers. What I do know is that their security is extraordinary. Those attack droids are programmed to shoot blaster fire. Not to stun, to kill."

Suddenly Mazara stopped and gave them a shrewd look. "Attack droids don't usually crash into each other."

"Yes, it's an unusual sight," Siri said.

She looked at them carefully. "I've traveled widely. I've seen enough to know you aren't workers. You took those droids down, didn't you?"

The Jedi said nothing, but Mazara nodded, as though they had confirmed her guess.

"You are Jedi," she said.

"Why do you say that?" Obi-Wan asked.

"There is word on the street that those who identify Jedi will be paid for it," she said. "Don't worry, you can trust me. What are you doing on Falleen? Have you come to help us?"

"We've come to investigate several of your facto-ries," Siri said carefully.

"That will help us, no matter what your purpose," Mazara said. "You can take word of what is happening back to the Galactic Senate."

Anakin exchanged a quick glance with Obi-Wan. He knew that like him, his Master had his doubts that the Senate would be able to stop what was going on here. The Senate was roiled with its own problems as the new movement of Separatists was fraying old loyalties and creating new alliances. Very little legislation was being enacted, and petitions for help from many worlds were delayed by procedure.

"Have you heard of someone called Granta Omega?" Obi-Wan asked casually.

Mazara shook her head.

"How about Roy Teda?"

"Yes, of course, the deposed dictator of Romin. He's here." Mazara grimaced. "Falleen seems to attract the worst of the galaxy, these days."

"Do you know where he is?" Siri asked.

"Of course. He's staying in the kind of reclusive hotel reserved for the ultra-rich. I learned about it back in my investigative days."

"Is he staying with anyone else?"

Mazara shook her head. "Not that I know of."

Obi-Wan glanced at Siri. Roy Teda and Zan Arbor had split up, most likely.

"You said that there were deaths at the Blackwater facility," Ferus pointed out.

Mazara nodded. "And rumors of sicknesses that cannot be diagnosed. Rumors that Falleen are forced to work in water tunnels. We are able to stay underwater for long periods of time."

"Water tunnels?" Obi-Wan asked.

Anakin felt a surge of excitement. So they were on the right track after all. They knew that Zan Arbor was trying to perfect the transmission of her Zone of Self-Containment through water.

"That wing of the factory is restricted. It's set up for transmission experiments," Mazara said. "Workers are forced to sign a statement of confidentiality, and so far, no one has dared to contest it. The penalties are unknown, but they must be severe."

"We would like to examine that wing," Obi-Wan said. "Can you get us inside the factory?"

"That is easy," Mazara said. "There are Falleen in the employment office who will help us. I can get you inside as workers. After that, the rest is up to you."

CHAPTER THREE

Mazara was as good as her word. She arranged an interview for Obi-Wan and Anakin that she promised would be a mere formality. Meanwhile, Siri and Ferus decided to stake out the exclusive hotel where Teda was staying and see what they could learn.

The four Jedi split up in the early morning. Their breath clouded from the cold air as they paused in the main square of the city to say good-bye.

"So how come I get to freeze on a factory floor while you hang around a luxury hotel?" Anakin grumbled good-naturedly to Ferus.

Ferus grinned. "Just lucky, I guess."

Obi-Wan was glad to see the ease between them. Ferus had unburdened himself on Romin and spoken to Obi-Wan of his fears about Anakin. Obi-Wan had been both irritated and alarmed by Ferus's insights. But it was as though passing along his worries had freed Ferus to unbend around Anakin. As a result, the tension between the two Padawans had lessened considerably.

"May the Force be with you," Siri told them.

Obi-Wan and Anakin headed off to join the river of workers crowding aboard cloud buses for the journey out to the Yellow District. They rode to the end of the line, then hiked the remaining distance. The other workers were silent, their faces gray and composed. The long, hard day lay in front of them.

Obi-Wan and Anakin went directly to the employment office. There, no questions were asked and they were given passes to the main factory floor by the employment officer, a Falleen named Wanuri.

"We are interested in working in the transmission wing," Obi-Wan told Wanuri as the Falleen pushed two security swipe cards across the desk to them.

Wanuri shook his head. "Can't do it, even for Mazara. Word has come down that no more workers are needed there. The night shift has been canceled, so everyone will be leaving exactly at six. The last hire always sweeps the factory floor. Be sure and lock the hydromop and repulsorbroom back in the utility closet. Here's the card. Be sure not to stay. Two security officers and droids make a sweep of the factory every fifteen minutes."

He pushed the card across the table. Obi-Wan pocketed it.

"Great," Anakin murmured as they headed to the factory floor. "Not only do we have to work all day, we have to clean up afterward."

"He gave us the job as a way to stay behind," Obi-Wan told Anakin. "We can hide somewhere until everyone leaves. He also told us how security is handled."

Obi-Wan and Anakin clipped the swipe cards to the front of their red unisuits, the uniform of the workers. They were given a manager to report to. He split them up into two different areas of the factory.

Obi-Wan took his place in a line of workers who were checking levels on machines that monitored the injection of liquid into small canisters. He could only assume that the Zone was packaged somehow within the canisters, but he didn't know if it was liquid or gas or some kind of suspended particles.

He was surprised at how disorganized the factory floor was. It was hard to tell what, exactly, was being manufactured. Each part of the factory was sealed off from the next, and Obi-Wan had no idea where the final product was being assembled.

Deep troughs were cut in the factory floor for the

waste, which was simply flushed down through the floors to outflow valves. If a worker stepped or fell into the trough by accident, he or she was coated in waste material. There was no way to know if the material was toxic. Unlike other factories, there were no decontamination rooms.

The work wasn't hard, just grindingly dull. The workers were used as a double-check to the machines, which rarely made errors.

The interesting thing to Obi-Wan was that supervision was light. A tier ran around the upper level of the vast space, where managers were supposed to monitor the workers below. But he noted that the managers rarely looked down. They were more concerned with eating, drinking tea, and joking with one another. There seemed to be no central authority making sure everything was getting done.

This worried Obi-Wan. It wasn't like either Omega or Zan Arbor to run a slipshod organization. Was he in the wrong place?

He confided his doubts to Anakin at the break. Anakin nodded.

"I've noticed the same thing, Master. My work partner said the managers all changed two weeks ago. The workers haven't had to work as hard. They're all relieved."

But Obi-Wan wasn't. He was uneasy.

"We're wasting time if this factory isn't preparing the Zone for use," Obi-Wan said.

"We'll find out tonight," Anakin said.

But would it be too late? Obi-Wan couldn't shake his uneasiness.

The rest of the day passed in repetition and drudgery. The workers were bored and worked at half speed, and none of the managers cared.

Before the end of the workday, Obi-Wan reported to the manager in order to clean the factory floor. Together with Anakin, they swept and mopped. There was no one to oversee them or make certain they did a good job. When the buzzer sounded, signaling the end of the workday, Obi-Wan and Anakin headed to a utility closet. They placed the repulsorbroom and hyrdomop inside. With a quick glance to make sure no one was watching, they ducked inside the closet, too.

The noises of the departing workers faded. They heard a lone security guard make his rounds. Then everything shut down at once. They heard the locks slam home on the doors outside. The tiny light in the closet shut off.

They waited a few minutes, listening intently for any movement outside the door. Then Obi-Wan opened the door carefully. They quickly moved down the hallway and peeked out on to the factory floor. The machines looked like sleeping creatures in the dim light.

"We have about eleven minutes before the droid sweep," Obi-Wan murmured. "Let's head for the wing."

They ran down the aisle, keeping an eye out for the security guard. They hurried to the door that led to the restricted wing.

Now they were faced with a double-coded lock.

"Our swipe card will work if we can override the code," Obi-Wan said. "We don't want to tip anyone off that we were here."

He worked at the keypad for several minutes.

"Master, the droid sweep."

Frustrated, Obi-Wan tried another combination. He had studied codes at the Temple with the great Jedi Master Nan Latourain, but this code was proving too difficult for him.

"Master!"

Obi-Wan jumped away as he heard the *whirr* of the droids. He and Anakin hid behind a gravsled as the droids swept by, their surveillance unit revolving steadily. As soon as they were gone, the Jedi re-emerged.

Obi-Wan attacked the keypad again.

"Let me try," Anakin suggested.

Obi-Wan stepped aside. He watched Anakin work. He felt Anakin call upon the Force. The Force grew around them, pulsing and shimmering, but the Force could not unlock keypads.

"We're stuck," Anakin said. "There has to be another way."

Obi-Wan felt the same uneasiness, the same sense of urgency, he had felt earlier today.

Suddenly in his mind, he saw Qui-Gon Jinn's easy smile.

You know the answer. Why don't you trust it?

Obi-Wan withdrew his lightsaber and slashed through the lock in one motion. The door swung open.

"Well, that's one way," Anakin commented.

They found themselves in a short hallway with another security door. Obi-Wan didn't hesitate this time, but buried his lightsaber in the durasteel. It peeled away in a glowing arc of light and smoke.

They hurried through. They were now in a large room that served as a laboratory. Anakin quickly headed to the console, where he thought the files might be kept. Obi-Wan made a survey of the room.

"There are valves here that go to tunnels," he told Anakin. "Big enough to walk in. I suspect that despite the laws, they experimented on the workers themselves."

"They did," Anakin said, reading from the files. "Different levels of the Zone. The four worker deaths were from overexposure. They were trying to calibrate exact amounts for large crowds. Thousands at once. This factory is definitely Omega's. Zan Arbor can't be far off."

Obi-Wan strode over to read over Anakin's shoulder.

"Zan Arbor had already perfected one-on-one transmission," Obi-Wan said. "But this indicates she's searching for a way to infect a whole city."

"So we were right," Anakin said. "The proof is in these files."

Obi-Wan pointed to the bottom of the file.

TRACK A EXPERIMENT VOIDED.

TRACK B EXPERIMENT BEGUN.

"Track A and Track B? I wonder what that means," he said.

"This science is over my head," Anakin said, flipping through the holofile. "We'll have to get inspectors in."

"We have enough evidence to go straight to the Supreme Chancellor," Obi-Wan said. "That's the only way things get done, these days."

Anakin looked at his chrono. "We have another six minutes before the next droid sweep."

"Let's check out the tunnel."

Quickly they opened the valve and stepped inside the tunnel. They walked down, using their glow rods for illumination. Vents were spaced evenly on the tunnel walls, and the plastoid sides were smooth.

Obi-Wan stepped over to the side and peered into a vent. "I see some ducts and hoses. This must be how the Zone is administered," he said. He stepped away to study a schematic drawing that was light-lasered onto the wall. Tunnels branched out from the main tunnel, and it appeared to be an extensive system.

"The tunnels go on for whole kilometers," Obi-Wan said, surprised. "Enough to approximate an entire small city, right here in the factory. This tunnel dips underground and joins the main system. It connects to other smaller tunnels. . . ."

Anakin cocked his head. "Master . . ."

"It's so detailed. I wonder if it's based on an actual city system. . . ."

"Master." Anakin's voice was urgent now.

Obi-Wan turned. "The droids? I doubt they sweep the tunnels."

"Not droids," Anakin said. "Water."

Obi-Wan whipped around just as a wall of water rushed down the tunnel. His feet were swept out from under him and he was propelled forward, smashing against the side of the tunnel and then somersaulting out of control against the power of the water. He fought his way to the surface, kicking and stroking. Once his head cleared, he saw Anakin nearby. They were careening down the tunnel with the force of the current.

"Aqua breathers!" Obi-Wan shouted.

He drew his out of his utility belt. Anakin did the same. At least they would not drown. But it would be impossible to fight their way back up the tunnel against the water. On the drawing, the tunnel seemed simply to end in bedrock. They would be smashed against it at this rate.

Then Obi-Wan heard a worse noise, one he hadn't expected. Fighting the pull of the water, he thrashed around until he was facing behind him, the way they had come. At first he could only see the wall of churning water, waves of it coming toward him. Then he realized what was happening.

The tunnel was imploding behind them. In another few seconds, they would be crushed in the collapse.

CHAPTER FOUR

Anakin saw the danger at the same time as his Master. He did not waste time worrying. His gaze raked the tunnel sides, looking for a way to escape, even as the torrent of water turned him end over end in a tumbling motion that left him dizzy.

Most of the vents were too small, but Anakin remembered something. He had glanced only briefly at the schematic plan, but he remembered a larger vent that came a quarter-kilometer from the end of the tunnel. It had connected to another tunnel that had seemed to come to a dead end. But it would have to do. That would be their only chance to escape the water. That is, if the side tunnels had not been flooded as well.

But how far had they traveled? Which vent was the right one?

Obi-Wan must have had the same thought, but Anakin's Master had studied the blueprint longer. "Anakin!" Obi-Wan shouted over the sound of the rushing water. "Vent coming up on the left, five hundred meters! Grab on!"

"All right!" Anakin yelled, and got a mouthful of water. Choking, he stroked to keep himself above water. He would need every bit of his strength. Dust and debris from the collapsing tunnel now filled the air, making it difficult to breathe. The roar was deafening. Underneath the flow of the water, Anakin felt something else — a deep shuddering, as though the ground itself was moving.

He saw his Master stroke against the water. Anakin fought through the torrent, kicking his legs, and pushing against the water with his arms. He could not make headway.

The Force bounced over the water. It came from his Master. Anakin used it as Obi-Wan intended. He was part of the water now. He could feel the spaces within the drops and was able to let the water break over him and find a way to move against it. He pushed with all his might, but his effort didn't cost him his strength. It doubled it.

He made headway against the water, reaching the side of the tunnel, immediately behind Obi-Wan. Now the trick would be to get inside the vent. His Master held his cable launcher aloft, over the foaming water, and Anakin saw his objective. He unhooked his launcher as well, keeping himself afloat with one hand as he was knocked against the tunnel wall.

Now the vent was coming toward them — fast, faster than he'd planned for. He saw Obi-Wan's launcher snake out and catch on the vent. Obi-Wan grabbed the cable, fighting his way back against the water. Anakin aimed at the metal grid of the vent and missed.

He called on the Force to help him even as he was swept down past the vent. He pushed against the water, feeling it break against his skin. He felt the spaces between the particles and slipped through them.

Fingers dug into his coveralls and pulled. Obi-Wan reached under his arm and yanked him forward. Anakin was able to grab on to Obi-Wan's cable and hauled himself the rest of the way.

He joined Obi-Wan, hooking his fingers into the grating. The pressure of the water held the vent in place. They pulled with all their strength as the water cascaded over their heads, sometimes submerging them completely. The tunnel behind them was collapsing, chunks of plastoid and durasteel falling into the churning water and sometimes slamming against them on its way.

The Force gathered and grew. The grating popped off, then bounced away on the rushing water.

Obi-Wan pushed Anakin inside the small space of the vent. Anakin slid forward as fast as he could pull himself, making room. His Master pulled himself up and in.

They panted for a moment, acknowledging the difficulty of the struggle. Then Obi-Wan quickly began to crawl forward.

"I see something ahead," he called. "A bit of gray light."

"Let's hope it's a way out."

Anakin followed his Master on his hands and knees. The small pipe they were crawling through was shaking now as the ground trembled around them.

Ahead he could now see that the blackness was faintly tinged with gray.

"There's a ladder."

He could hear the relief in his Master's voice. Anakin looked up. A metal ladder rose vertically and disappeared into the blackness above. Obi-Wan began to climb.

Anakin followed. A sudden blast of debris roared

through the pipe below and rose toward them. He tasted dirt and metal in his mouth and choked.

He couldn't speak. He coughed out the debris in his mouth and kept climbing. He knew the pipe was collapsing below. At any moment they could be buried underground.

Obi-Wan suddenly stopped. He knocked on something over his head. "It's layers of durasteel," he said, struggling to reach for his lightsaber in the tiny space. "I'll have to cut through."

Anakin knew they had barely any time left. He watched as Obi-Wan buried his lightsaber in the metal plating above. The ladder was hot under his hands. It began to peel away from the side of the pipe. The system was collapsing.

Suddenly another stream of light joined Obi-Wan's from above. Anakin saw the durasteel peel away. Then Siri's face appeared. "You'd better hurry," she said.

"That's the general idea," Obi-Wan answered, scrambling up the ladder.

Anakin followed as the ladder began to melt beneath him. He grabbed on to Siri's strong grip and threw himself toward the opening. He was half pulled, half hauled up to the surface. He lay flat on the ground, breathing heavily.

"Come on," Siri urged in his ear. "We have to get out of here. The entire factory is imploding."

Anakin could feel the ground moving beneath him. He rose and began to run with the others. Ferus was in the lead, dashing over the ground even as it pitched and heaved. It was like running across a turbulent air current.

They reached the safety of the open plain and turned back to look. It was an amazing sight. The ground simply cracked apart in chunks and opened up. It swallowed the huge factory and caved in with a shower of fire and dust. Within only minutes, there was a smoking crater where the factory had been.

All the evidence had been sucked into the ground. Not even debris remained.

"We came to find you," Siri said. "We saw the beginning of the collapse. We knew you would be inside the wing, so we raced around the perimeter, looking for a way in. The Force led me to the spot and then I sighted your lightsaber."

"Omega knew we were here," Anakin said, gazing at the crater. "He destroyed the factory to silence us and to cover his tracks."

"Teda has left the planet," Siri said.

"We fear Omega and Zan Arbor went with him," Ferus added. "They didn't file a flight plan. There's no way of knowing where in the galaxy they are headed."

Anakin saw his Master's jaw tighten. He knew Obi-

Wan was at the end of his control. He could feel the frustration coiled inside him. Once again, Granta Omega had escaped.

Obi-Wan's comlink signaled. He glanced at it. "It's Master Windu," he said in a tight voice.

They all waited a moment. Anakin watched his Master curiously. He knew Obi-Wan was fighting the temptation to throw the comlink into the vast area of the plains.

"Maybe you should answer it," Siri suggested in a soft voice Anakin had never heard before. She was gazing at Obi-Wan with concern in her deep blue eyes.

Obi-Wan pressed the holomode on his comlink.

Mace Windu appeared in miniature holographic form. "Obi-Wan, Siri. The Jedi teams must return to Coruscant immediately."

"But we are on the trail of Granta Omega," Obi-Wan said. "We just —"

"Immediately," Mace interrupted. "There is trouble."

CHAPTER FIVE

Mace Windu was too busy to meet the two teams in the Council Room, or one of the smaller meeting rooms. They had to catch up to him as he strode down the Great Hall on his way to a Senate meeting.

He did not ask them how their pursuit of Granta Omega was going, or how their journey had been. Obi-Wan was relieved. The answers to both of those questions would have been negative. He felt fatigue shudder along his bones, and he knew both Ferus and Anakin, who were walking a few steps behind, needed rest. There did not seem to be much rest for any of the Jedi, these days.

"A feeling of distrust toward the Jedi Council has been growing among certain Senators," Mace said as he walked purposefully, his robe swinging with the motion. "We have felt it for some time. We were not overly concerned. We knew Senators like Sano Sauro undermined us whenever they could. Lately, things have escalated. A faction is now active; it has influence. The Jedi Council senses that there is someone behind this faction, but we don't know who it is."

Obi-Wan looked at Siri incredulously. They had been called back to the Temple because of a Senate *power struggle*? There were few things that interested him less.

"False stories have been spread," Mace continued. "Events have been twisted so that the Jedi are seen as disloyal to the Republic, as interfering in galactic political matters by making them worse."

"Master Windu," Obi-Wan said carefully, "you have called us off an important mission to find a great enemy —"

"I know exactly what I did, Obi-Wan," Mace said. "A powerful enemy outside and powerful enemies within. Can you decide who is more deadly?"

"But a Senate power struggle . . . is not unusual," Obi-Wan protested, trying to keep his composure under the glare of Mace's penetrating eyes.

Mace stopped so abruptly that his robe swung around like a whip. He looked at each of the Jedi, and seemed to pick up the fatigue and frustration there. He hesitated a moment.

"I recognize the importance of your mission," he said gravely. "But your mission is one of hundreds, which all involve peacekeeping, saving lives, helping governments, fostering alliances. The Jedi are involved in missions throughout the galaxy, which will be compromised if this faction is not dealt with."

"What do you mean? How could one faction in the Senate harm thousands of Jedi?" Siri asked.

"By organizing the withdrawal of official Senate support for the Jedi Council," Mace said. He let his words settle over them.

"You understand what this would mean," he continued, when he was sure he had their complete attention. "To operate without Senate approval would make us rogue diplomats and would completely undercut our authority. In short, without Senate support the effectiveness of the Jedi will be decimated."

"But why did you call *us* back to fight this?" Anakin asked.

Ferus glanced at Anakin, amazed. Obi-Wan had to admit that the question did sound more like a complaint than a query.

Mace settled his severe gaze on Anakin. Obi-Wan thought that Anakin was most likely the only Jedi apprentice who could take it without flinching. Most

Padawans seemed to visibly shrink as Master Windu's eyes plumbed their depths, seeming to find every petty motivation, every secret weakness they had.

Anakin merely waited. Strong, graceful, sure of himself.

"I chose this team because of your special skills," Mace told Anakin. "Obi-Wan may hate it, but he has a great knowledge of the Senate workings. I contacted Yoda on Kashyyyk, and he was in agreement."

Obi-Wan tried not to groan aloud. Siri allowed herself one small smile at his discomfort.

"His contacts are invaluable," Mace went on. "I chose Master Tachi for her lack of patience."

Siri's small grin disappeared. Mace raised an eyebrow at her.

"A fault she has tried to correct, but one that often gets in her way," he said. "I have a feeling it will be useful in this situation. Senators are used to deference. Without it, they feel lost. I wouldn't mind some of them feeling a bit unbalanced. And Ferus, of course, is a worthy addition. He studied Senate structure and knows more about it than any apprentice. And you, Anakin . . ."

Anakin waited.

"You have two things that can help us. One, of

course, is your Force connection. You are just beginning to realize how it can work on beings as well as objects."

Anakin looked startled, as if he didn't understand that anyone else knew this. Obi-Wan suddenly realized it was true, and that he had known it without acknowledging it. How had Mace Windu discovered this? He had been with the group on Romin for only a short time.

Well. That was why Mace was on the Jedi Council. That was why, except for Yoda, Obi-Wan thought him the most powerful Jedi he'd ever known.

"Yes, together with observation and intuition the Force can help you see into the hearts and minds of others," Mace said softly, his eyes not leaving Anakin's face. "That is why the Force must be respected and handled with care."

"I know that, Master Windu," Anakin said.

"Perhaps you do. Or perhaps you will learn it more with every mission, the way the rest of us do. And there is one other thing," Mace said, resuming his walk. "Chancellor Palpatine has asked to see you and Obi-Wan specifically. He has requested a meeting."

Obi-Wan felt his heart sink. Most likely it would be the first of many meetings in the Senate, where it would be explained to him why the simplest way to do things was actually the most complicated.

"When is the meeting?" Obi-Wan asked, trying not to sigh as he matched his walk to Mace's long stride.

For the first time, Mace's features softened, and Obi-Wan was almost sure he caught the slightest of smiles. "Do not fret, Obi-Wan. You are on your way to it."

CHAPTER SIX

Anakin and Obi-Wan stood in the reception room outside Supreme Chancellor Palpatine's private offices in the Senate. They stayed by the window, looking out at the busy space lanes, while Siri and Ferus took up positions near the door and Mace, with the utmost calmness, took a chair.

"I know how disappointed you are, Master," Anakin said.

"Master Windu is right," Obi-Wan replied. "We are needed here. And besides . . ."

The pause continued. Anakin waited for his Master to finish the sentence, but Obi-Wan continued to stare out at the airspeeders jockeying for position. Some were coming to dock at the vast landing platform that served the Senate. Anakin watched them for a moment as well. If the Senators or their underlings could not obey traffic rules on when to yield and when to go, how could they solve the problems of the galaxy?

"On Romin, do you remember how Teda said they would be going to Coruscant?" Obi-Wan said at last. "We couldn't decide if that was a diversion or not."

"We didn't think Teda was clever enough to create a diversion," Anakin said with a grin.

"Exactly. What is happening here . . . it has the marks of Omega on it."

Anakin was startled. "Do you think Omega is involved in the movement to discredit the Jedi?"

"I don't know. Maybe not directly, but it's best to keep it in mind. It certainly fits his interests, doesn't it? Maybe returning here was not an end to our journey, but a continuation."

Sly Moore slipped out from the interior room with silent grace. She nodded at the waiting Jedi to indicate that Chancellor Palpatine was ready to receive them, then lifted one slender arm draped in silvery fabric to indicate the door they should take.

Siri, Ferus, Obi-Wan, Anakin, and Mace entered the inner office.

Palpatine stood by a grouping of chairs. Anakin thought he looked imposing in his simple robes of muted colors. His face looked pale and drawn, almost bloodless. Anakin imagined that the Chancellor's job robbed him of rest and outdoor activity. He was sacrificing his life in order to save the Senate from being overrun by those who would use it for their own ends.

"I am indebted to you for coming so promptly," Palpatine greeted them in the deep voice whose softness served to convey his power. "Please sit. There is no time to lose."

He waited until the Jedi were all seated before sitting himself. Palpatine shook his head, as if in deep thought. "I feel such sorrow for having to bring you here," he said. "I am ashamed of the Senate. There is a growing tide of anti-Jedi feeling and the best of us cannot seem to stop it. It is full of lies and half-truths, all twisted to fit an agenda." Palpatine opened his palms in a gesture of helplessness. "I am at a loss to explain it, except to say that in a galaxy so mired in conflict some might turn to a scapegoat to further their own plans."

"Or deflect attention from those plans," Mace said.

"That is true, Master Windu," Palpatine said. "And wise. But what these plans are, I do not know."

"Is Sano Sauro behind this?" Obi-Wan asked. Senator Sauro was an enemy of the Jedi, and Omega had been his protégé as a boy.

Palpatine shook his head. "Not this time. The

leader of the anti-Jedi faction is a formerly obscure Senator from Nuralee. His name is Bog Divinian."

Obi-Wan started. Bog Divinian! He was married to Obi-Wan's good friend Astri Oddo, the daughter of Didi Oddo. Obi-Wan had met Bog on a mission during the Galactic Games. Bog was not yet a Senator at that time, but he had lied in his testimony to an official investigation in order to protect the Commerce Guild. Obi-Wan had no doubt then that Bog had the makings of a politician. He was not surprised to hear he had succeeded in his career. No doubt the gratitude of the powerful Commerce Guild had helped.

Obi-Wan glanced at Mace. Now he knew there was another reason he had been called to help.

"I know Bog Divinian," he said. "His wife is an old friend."

Palpatine looked relieved. "That is good news. I urge you to speak directly to him. Perhaps a personal appeal can help."

Obi-Wan doubted this was the case, but he inclined his head in agreement.

"I must inform you of a recent development," Palpatine said. "Roy Teda has arrived on Coruscant. I know that the Jedi were recently involved in the coup on his planet of Romin."

Obi-Wan felt this news pass like electricity between

him and the other Jedi. Perhaps his idea about Omega being involved here wasn't so far-fetched.

"Teda has lost no time in joining the anti-Jedi faction, I'm afraid," Palpatine continued. "He's already given testimony that the Jedi were responsible for aiding the unlawful coup on his planet."

"Unfortunately this is technically true, though a misreading of events," Mace said, arching an eyebrow at Obi-Wan. Obi-Wan knew that Mace was still annoyed at him and Siri for aiding a coup without first consulting the Jedi Council.

But Teda's arrival on the planet could be good news, Obi-Wan thought. It would give them a chance to observe him closely. Perhaps they could learn more about Omega. Teda was not a bright creature, and no doubt it would be possible to discover how he fit into Omega's larger plans.

"He has also claimed that the Jedi were responsible for a factory implosion on Falleen. He's managed to get the Falleen Senator quite upset about it." Chancellor Palpatine steepled his fingers and looked over them at the Jedi. "I'm afraid there is nothing I can do about this. There is just enough evidence in the charges to make them credible. Teda has the right to petition for asylum on Coruscant. It is up to the Jedi Council to refute the charges."

"Are the charges formal?" Mace asked, somewhat surprised.

"Yes. That is the reason for this meeting. There will be a hearing this afternoon. I suggest that a Jedi presence is needed."

Mace stood. "Master Kenobi will attend the hearing."

"He must," Palpatine said. "He has been called as a witness."

Once again, Obi-Wan inclined his head, but he seethed inwardly at the distraction. *Just my luck,* he thought. *A meeting and a Senate hearing, all in the same day.*

Omega could be in his grasp, but if he wasn't careful, he would spend all his time in meetings and hearings and never accomplish a thing.

Just like a Senator, Obi-Wan thought with an inward groan.

CHAPTER SEVEN

The hearing was held in a smaller meeting room at the Senate. It wasn't as big as the main chamber, but it held twenty tiers with seating for onlookers and pods for several hundred Senators. The room was packed with an overflow crowd. Senators, aides, HoloNet news correspondents, and curious Coruscant natives crowded the seats and the aisles in the tiers, and every pod was full.

Obi-Wan sat in a pod with Mace Windu, docked in a mid-level tier. "I'm surprised there is such a crowd for this hearing," he murmured to Mace. "Usually meetings like this are so dull that no one attends."

"Note who is here," Mace said in a low tone. "The room is packed with Bog Divinian's supporters. I hear

that one must obtain tickets to observe, and supporters of the Jedi were told there were no seats."

Obi-Wan watched as Bog Divinian leaned forward to
call Roy Teda to the stand. Teda's pod floated forward.

"I greet you hello, fellow rulers, amazing Senators,
all wonderful beings who love democracy and truth,"
Roy Teda said. "I, too, am a believer and a lover of the
democratic principles of many voices, all saying the
same thing."

Roy Teda began his testimony, and began to lie.

Obi-Wan listened to the lies fall from his mouth. He
was not surprised.

"I beseech you, Senators, rulers, fellow citizens of
the galaxy," Teda concluded, spreading his arms. "Stop
this outrageous outrage before it overtakes us completely! The Jedi came to my planet and secretly plotted
in an underhanded way with an unlawful army to bring
about the destruction of the elected government!"

Obi-Wan snorted. "Hardly an army," he said quietly
to Mace. "And we didn't plot with them."

"The truth has no place here," Mace replied. "They
don't want to hear it. But you must tell your truth anyway."

"They overthrew my government! They rampaged
through the streets! And it is no accident," Teda said,

leaning forward on his fists, "that the Romin treasury of wealth disappeared!"

"Yes, because you looted it," Obi-Wan muttered.

"Jedi interference must be outlawed on every planet in the galaxy!" Teda thundered. "Let them go back to their Temple and practice their secret hidden arts on one another!" he shouted. "Leave governing the galaxy to the Senate!"

Blocs of Senators roared approval. The crowd hooted and stamped.

High above Teda, Bog Divinian hovered. He did not dock his pod the way the presiding Senator usually did. He remained in midair, so that he would be in full view of the crowd.

"Senator Divinian, I have signaled for questioning and have been ignored!" Bail Organa's voice was a shout. He stood, maneuvering his pod closer to Bog's.

"If you have a question, of course the presiding official — which is me, may I remind you — will recognize it," Bog said, clearly displeased at the interruption. "The Honorable Senator from Alderaan has the floor."

Organa's pod zoomed closer. "Do you have any evidence of your claims, Former Ruler Teda?" he asked. His handsome face was stern, and his robes were thrown back off his shoulders as he faced the former dictator.

"Yes, of course," Teda answered smoothly. "The evidence is on Romin, only I am in exile and cannot reach it."

"The committee has ruled that a subcommittee will be formed in order to investigate the charges," Bog announced.

"And who will be appointed to this subcommittee?" Organa asked, turning to Bog.

"Some members of my committee —"

"All enemies of the Jedi!" Organa thundered.

"— who will choose its members, according to rule 729900, subsection B38 of the subcommittee rules —"

"— which are currently being revised by a committee headed by Senator Sano Sauro, another enemy of the Jedi!" Organa pointed out. There were few Senators who studied the bureaucracy as extensively. Organa knew that the tedious work of keeping up with the bureaucracy netted results. Injustice often began when the powerful Senators who headed committees changed obscure rules that they knew no one would notice.

No one but Bail Organa.

"The Honorable Senator from Alderaan must agree that no matter how unhappy he may be, it cannot be argued that procedure isn't being followed," Bog said smugly.

"The procedure was changed by the same Senator who has been asked to investigate unfounded charges that suit his own agenda," Organa pointed out. "It is the very definition of unfair. It is also an outrage."

Obi-Wan was impressed. Organa spoke with authority. He did not bluster or shout. He made his points with acid, not with blows. He spoke truth, but Mace was right — this crowd did not want to hear it.

"The presiding official refuses to get bogged down in procedural details," Bog said, waving his hand. "The Honorable Senator from Alderaan will now yield the floor. Your objections will be noted in the log. The presiding official calls Jedi Knight Obi-Wan Kenobi for testimony."

Obi-Wan stood at the front of his pod. He pressed the lever that controlled its movement. The box moved forward to the center of the room.

Bog did not acknowledge that he knew Obi-Wan or had met him before, not even with a slight nod.

"Tell us, Jedi Kenobi, did the Jedi secretly meet with the resistance army on Romin?"

"Members of the resistance movement captured two of our apprentices," Obi-Wan replied. "The Jedi were on Romin to pursue a galactic criminal —"

"Ah, let's talk about that. Isn't it true you were on Romin illegally and using false ID docs?"

"It is true that we used false ID docs. Sometimes the Jedi need to travel in secrecy," Obi-Wan answered.

"We were on the trail of an extremely dangerous criminal who had the means to destroy —"

"I am not asking your intent, merely clarifying your means," Bog interrupted. "Which, as I pointed out, were against the laws of Romin. Did you have personal dealings with the criminal Joylin who has seized power on Romin?"

"An action that the Senate sanctioned due to the criminal activities of Roy Teda," Obi-Wan pointed out.

"There are some in the Senate who pushed through this initiative, it's true," Bog said, implying that this action was highly suspect. "That initiative is currently under investigation."

"Senator Divinian!" Bail Organa called.

"Senator Organa, you are out of order!" Bog thundered. "I am questioning this witness!" He turned back to Obi-Wan. "Answer the question. Isn't it true that the Jedi assisted the takeover?"

Obi-Wan hesitated a fraction of a second. It was true that the Jedi did assist Joylin and his band. But the plans had already been in place.

"Answer, please." Obi-Wan saw a flash of mean triumph in Bog's eyes.

"Yes. We offered them assistance."

"So you overthrew a legally elected government for your own purposes."

"No. We —"

"The record will note that the question has been answered," Bog snapped.

Bog looked down at his datapad, but Obi-Wan was sure it was for show. Bog knew exactly what his next question was going to be. He wanted Obi-Wan's admission to hang in the air. The chamber was silent now, every face turned toward Obi-Wan. He was in an impossible position, and he knew it. He could not save the Jedi here. He could not save the Jedi with words, with truth.

Obi-Wan rarely felt helpless. He hated the feeling. He felt it burn inside.

"Isn't it also true that the Jedi were involved in a factory implosion on Falleen?"

"We happened to be in the vicinity."

"Oh," sneered Bog, "Jedi Knights are factory workers now?"

"Two of us were," Obi-Wan answered honestly.

"Do you mean to tell me that you got jobs in a factory? That's hard to believe."

"Truth is sometimes hard to believe," Obi-Wan said evenly. "That's why ignorant minds have a difficult time with it."

Bog's face reddened. Obi-Wan realized he had done

an ignorant thing himself. He had allowed his temper to get the better of his judgment. Always a bad idea — and, for a Jedi, a severe lapse.

"So you sabotaged the factory —"

"No." It was Obi-Wan's turn to interrupt. "We were caught there. The factory was deliberately destroyed by its owner to cover up violations."

"And you were there, after hours, after everyone else had gone home."

"Yes."

"I see. So you were the only ones there during the implosion, but you did not trigger it."

"I don't know if we were the only ones there. How do you?"

Bog flushed again. "What I see before me is arrogance and a complete lack of remorse at the destruction of property —"

"Oh, I feel remorse," Obi-Wan said.

"That is unusual," Bog snapped.

"I never received my paycheck."

Guffaws exploded throughout the chamber. Bog looked helpless and angry. Obi-Wan followed his gaze to a dark corner of the chamber, where a pod hugged the wall. Obi-Wan recognized the slim, dark form of Sano Sauro.

Sauro must have sent Bog a private message on his datapad, for Bog looked down. He nodded vigorously, while the laughter slowly died down.

Obi-Wan had succeeded in something, at least. He knew now that Sano Sauro was controlling Bog like a puppet.

"The witness is dismissed," Bog said. "The hearing is adjourned."

Obi-Wan maneuvered the pod back to the wall. He crossed to sit next to Mace. "I'm sorry."

"Don't be, Obi-Wan. You did the best you could."

Mace looked out over the chamber crowded with beings. "Something is here," he murmured. "Some darkness. We feel it growing, but every time we look, we see nothing at all. You spend your time on missions, Obi-Wan. You are not here, like the Jedi Council is. Lately, I have been wondering . . ."

"Yes, Master Windu?" Obi-Wan asked respectfully. It wasn't often that Mace revealed what he was thinking.

"We send the Jedi throughout the galaxy. To help. To keep peace. To bring aid to suffering populations. But in the end, I wonder . . ." Mace's stubborn gaze raked the chamber ". . . if our real job lies here."

"I hope not," Obi-Wan said, gazing over the room. "Out of all my missions, this is one place where I do not want to stand and fight. It's like shouting into the wind."

"None of us want to be here, Obi-Wan," Mace said. "Perhaps that is our undoing."

He took a step back, then turned and disappeared into the interior hallways. Obi-Wan looked out over the crowded chamber. How, he wondered, had it come to this? Why were so many willing to believe the worst of the Jedi Order?

He glanced over at the shadowy box where Sano Sauro sat, receiving guests. Obi-Wan had first tangled with Sauro as a mere boy, when Sauro had questioned him in a hearing to investigate the accidental death of a student at the Jedi Temple. Sauro had twisted Obi-Wan's words even then, and Obi-Wan suspected that the Senator had crafted Bog's questions today.

Disgusted, Obi-Wan turned and headed out of the box toward the interior reception room, where most of the crowd was now congregating. He saw Bog Divinian hurrying toward him, a wide smile on his face.

"Obi-Wan! So good to see you again!" Bog thumped him on the shoulder. Obi-Wan gazed at him incredulously.

"Oh, you didn't mind my questions, did you? Politics. A rough game, eh? I hope there are no hard feelings. After all, politics is temporary. Friendship is for-ever."

Obi-Wan just stared at him. Friendship? With Bog? They had never been friends. Bog's words were completely hollow, as empty as the man before him.

"Oh, excuse me, I forgot." Bog whipped out a small data recorder. "Hearing ended, great success, now greeting supporters."

Bog indicated the recorder to Obi-Wan. "This is how I keep track of things. And one day it will come in handy when my biography is written. You'd be shocked and dismayed if you knew how many important leaders neglected to keep notes and records for the biographer to follow."

Obi-Wan said nothing. Whereas once he bowed and scraped to please those in power in order to advance his career, now Bog saw himself as a great leader. He had fulfilled his early promise and become a pompous, scheming bore.

Bog rode over Obi-Wan's silence. "Have you seen my wife? She's here. She is dying to see you." Bog searched above the crowd, then began to wave. "Astri! Astri! I found our friend!"

Obi-Wan saw Astri then. She was dressed in a simple blue robe, but her carriage was regal, and she looked as impressive as the Senators and their entourages who were dressed in opulent cloaks. She had cut her springy curls short, clipped to fall softly around her head. She came toward him slowly through the crowd, not rushing, as Astri always used to do. Her gaze seemed to slide off him in the way that he had come to know from other officials — diplomats, Senators, rulers — those who met beings constantly and never invested in a true exchange of hearts and minds with any of them. His heart fell in disappointment. Astri, he feared, had become a Senator's wife.

"Hello, Obi-Wan." Her voice was pitched lower, yet another thing that had changed. "I'm glad to see you looking so well."

"I'm glad to see you, too," Obi-Wan said, even though he realized that Astri hadn't really said she was glad to see him. "And how is Didi?"

"He is back home." At last a small smile appeared on Astri's face, and he saw a flash of the prettiness he'd known. "Entertaining his grandson. Or should I say, they are entertaining each other."

Obi-Wan smiled. "You have a son?"

"A beautiful boy. His name is Lune. He just turned three."

"My son is the light of our lives," Bog said. "Astri, my dear, I fear that Obi-Wan is a little put out with me."

Astri's gaze lost its warmth and formality clicked

back into place. She looked away, past Obi-Wan's shoulder, into the crowd.

"You must tell him that each of us must follow our convictions," Bog continued.

"Obi-Wan knows this, no doubt."

"You must tell him how I've struggled with my decision to throw my support behind this. But I've come to feel that the Jedi Council wields too much influence in the Senate and with the Chancellor. I don't want to make enemies, I'm just looking for a more balanced approach. Is that so strange?"

Obi-Wan didn't answer. It was clear Bog did not expect one, and would not listen if one were given. The words he spoke seemed to have been memorized, crafted by someone far smarter than Bog.

How had Astri fallen for him? Obi-Wan had known Astri since he was a boy. He had watched her brave blaster fire and bounty hunters even while being terrified. All in order to save her father and Qui-Gon. She had turned herself from a cook in a rundown café into a warrior.

Now she was a Senator's wife. He felt sadness deep within him. Did he even know her anymore? Had everything, for Astri, only been about playing a role?

"It was nice to see you again, Obi-Wan," Astri said. "Take care."

She drifted off into the crowd. Bog gazed after her with affection.

"A perfect Senator's wife. She's involved in relief efforts, which is so important for my profile."

Obi-Wan felt he'd had enough. He saw Roy Teda leave a group of supporters and make his way toward the door. Saying a crisp farewell to Bog, Obi-Wan followed him. He had wasted enough time.

CHAPTER EIGHT

Anakin sat with Supreme Chancellor Palpatine in his red-walled office. Red Guards stood outside at attention. He had wanted to see how his Master did at the hearing, but Palpatine had detained him, and he couldn't refuse the Chancellor. How could you refuse someone whose term as Chancellor had expired years ago, but who stayed on to serve because so many saw him as integral to the well-being of the galaxy?

Anakin would have preferred to be searching the galaxy for Granta Omega, but he couldn't do that, either. There were times Anakin felt that wherever he turned, there was yet another order he could not refuse. He was trapped in everybody else's needs but his own.

Palpatine seemed to sense his mood. "You think you are wasting your time here," he observed.

Anakin searched for a way to be honest without being rude. "We were on an important mission."

"I can understand being frustrated by the Senate," Palpatine replied. "Yet here is where the power lies."

"It is not power I'm interested in," Anakin said.

"Really." The former Senator from Naboo smiled. "That is a very Jedi-like response. Yet, can I say this — it is not entirely true. The Jedi do not seek power, yet they have it. Why is that?"

The words sounded oddly familiar to him, as if he'd heard them before, but Anakin could not figure out where. He had a feeling that Palpatine was posing the question just to hear what Anakin had to say.

"Because we have the Force," Anakin said. "It is a source of power, yet we do not seek it. It is simply there."

"And it is a Jedi's choice to use it," Palpatine said.

Anakin smiled. "You sound almost like one of our critics."

"Hardly. I am the Jedi Council's biggest supporter. What I am trying to do is discover a way to fight those who seek to take away their power, their influence. I have come to several conclusions, though, and they aren't helpful. Would you care to hear them?"

"Of course." Anakin leaned forward slightly to show his interest. He felt flattered that Palpatine took him seriously enough to talk to him this way. He had imagined that the Chancellor did not waste his time with mere Padawan learners. He dealt directly with the Jedi Council, with powerful Jedi like Mace Windu and Yoda.

Palpatine looked out his window toward the spires of the Jedi Temple. His gaze was clouded. "One reason that the Jedi Order has become the object of jealousy in the Senate is that the Jedi don't know how to defend themselves. Of course the Jedi are bold warriors, but when it comes to the war of words in the Senate, they simply disengage. This is a grave mistake."

"Our actions and our results speak for themselves."

"There you are wrong. Results do not speak for themselves, not in the Senate. There must always be someone to *explain* why the results are good." Palpatine shrugged. "Everything must be interpreted, or someone else will do the interpreting. Facts are not important, only the twist that helps the Senators understand them. It is the way it is. They must be fed their diet of truth."

"You make Senators sound like children," Anakin observed.

"Ah, but they are." Palpatine shook his head. "I did not seek this office, yet I must carry out the burden of carrying on its duties. One of these duties is to recognize that what the Senate needs is a strong hand, just as children do."

"The Jedi don't believe that," Anakin argued. "In the Jedi Order, children are given the freedom to dissent and be independent."

Palpatine smiled. "Unlike the Jedi, Senators are not gifted with the Force. Jedi can afford to give their younglings freedom, because they know they are exceptional. Most beings are not exceptional, Anakin. They need someone to tell them what to do, and sometimes, what to believe."

Anakin struggled to grasp this. It went against what he believed. Yet he could not deny that Palpatine's strong hand had kept the Senate together during these years of growing strife with the Separatist movement.

"You want to turn the Jedi into politicians," he finally said.

"No. I want them to recognize that they are politicians, whether they like it or not. Power and politics are inseparable." Chancellor Palpatine rose. "You, Anakin Skywalker, you have power. I can see it in you. Your connection to the Force gives you clarity and boldness. The Jedi Order needs more like you."

"I am still a student," Anakin said, standing.

"Then learn," Palpatine told him. "Take this opportunity. Find out how to maneuver in Senate politics. It might turn out to be the skill the Jedi Council needs most. Not exactly the glory of lightsaber battles, but crucial nonetheless."

"How can I do that?" Anakin asked.

"Come with me to meetings while you're here," Palpatine said. "Watch. Listen. Tell me what you think, and I will share my thoughts with you."

It was an extraordinary offer. Anakin knew he had to take it.

"I will have to request permission from my Master."

Palpatine inclined his head. "Of course. And in the end, who knows? Perhaps you'll be able to teach Master Kenobi a thing or two."

CHAPTER NINE

Obi-Wan trailed Teda through the maze of Senate corridors that led through the various wings. He hated how Teda strolled as though he belonged there. He remembered the prison he had seen on Romin, the prisoners ragged and starving. He remembered the slums he had seen on the outskirts of the capital city, the luxury of Teda's life compared to the suffering he pushed outside the city walls. Teda did not deserve his clear conscience. He did not deserve his ease.

Teda stopped at last at one of the little cafés that were tucked into the alcoves of the Senate hallways, a place for beings to stop and take light refreshment before returning to their duties. Teda hesitated at the entrance and looked around, then headed to a table in a far corner. Obi-Wan headed for the self-service refreshment bar. As he helped himself to some tea, he saw in the mirror overhead that Teda was meeting Senator Sauro.

Obi-Wan made no attempt to conceal himself. He put down his steaming mug and headed to their table.

"I can't say this is a surprise," he said. "I expected that you would be behind any plot to discredit the Jedi Order, Sauro."

"As usual, you begin every exchange with rudeness," Sano Sauro said coolly. His thin face looked as tidy and pale as ever. His lips were almost white. He was dressed in a severe suit of black cloth. "I don't know what I've done to deserve your contempt and I don't care, but it continues to be tedious to put up with it."

"You know very well what you've done in the past, and what you are doing right now," Obi-Wan said. "You are the shadow behind these hearings."

Sauro sipped at a glass of water, the only item in front of him. "Senator Divinian is the presiding official over the hearings, not me."

"How odd, then, that you are meeting with the main witness against the Jedi," Obi-Wan said.

"I'm merely holding out a friendly hand to an exiled ruler of a democratic government that was overthrown by Jedi aggression," Sauro answered.

"That's right," Roy Teda said, anxious to demonstrate his importance in the discussion.

"Also, how odd that you chose to meet so far away from the hearing chamber, in a deserted part of the Senate," Obi-Wan remarked.

"I like peace and quiet," Sauro said. "Obviously, I am not finding it at the moment."

"That's exactly right," Teda repeated, nodding. He looked desperately eager to please Sano Sauro.

Sauro didn't pay attention to Teda. He kept his cool gaze on Obi-Wan. "So you see, Kenobi, I have no hand in the utter demoralization of the Jedi. I am merely a witness to it."

Obi-Wan leaned over the table on his fists. He locked eyes with Sauro. "I'll leave you to your thieves and murderers, Sauro. I realize they've gotten you far, but one day the company you keep will ensure your downfall."

"Who are you calling a murderer?" Teda sputtered. "Or wait, am I the thief?"

Obi-Wan turned on his heel and left. He walked quickly through the halls and jumped into a turbolift. He didn't want to waste any more time. He needed to talk to the one being he knew had the most knowledge of Senate intrigue, the best political mind he knew — his friend Tyro Caladian.

He took the lift down to the lowest level, then followed a twisting corridor that narrowed as it descended. After a short ramp, it turned and Obi-Wan found himself in a dim hallway. Bins and durasteel boxes were stacked outside a door. He smiled. Tyro hadn't changed a bit. He could always count on his industry.

The door was slightly ajar, so he pushed it open and peered in. "Tyro, I need you once again."

A voice came from behind a stack of procedural manuals. "My ears are happy! It is the voice of my friend Obi-Wan!"

A Svivreni poked his head over the manuals. His small face twitched and his bright eyes were alight with pleasure. He scurried out from behind the desk that took up almost the entire room. He stopped directly in front of Obi-Wan, opened his hand, and closed it. He placed it against his heart, and then Obi-Wan's.

Obi-Wan followed the same gestures. Svivreni had different codes of greeting and good-bye, and Obi-Wan had advanced to the most affectionate with Tyro. "It's been too long."

"Yes, indeed. Oh, let me find you a chair." Tyro broke away and began to sweep books off a chair. "You Jedi, never sitting, always moving."

Obi-Wan sat. Tyro leaned against the desk to face him. Now, they were eye to eye.

"I do not have to ask why you have come," Tyro said, his dark eyes full of worry. "I was at the hearing."

Obi-Wan grimaced. "I did badly."

"You did well, my friend. As did Senator Organa. But the anti-Jedi faction had packed the house with supporters. And Divinian's questioning!" Tyro threw up his hands. "An outrage. It was obvious he wasn't looking for truth. In another time, *too* obvious. Steps would be taken to have him removed from a position of authority. But these days . . ." Tyro shrugged and fiddled with the metal clasp that kept back his waist-length dark hair. It was a gesture he used when nervous, and Tyro was often anxious about the state of the Senate.

"Yes, things continue to decline, no matter how the Chancellor tries," Obi-Wan remarked.

"He does his best. But this uproar against the Jedi — I've never seen anything like it. Even for the Senate, it's ridiculous. And frustrating. It's just a distraction from the real work they should be doing."

Distraction. The word clanged like a bell inside his mind, but Obi-Wan didn't know why. Another word had hit him earlier, just a tiny *ping,* what was it . . .

Demoralized. Sauro had said that the Jedi were demoralized.

Disruption + Demoralization + Distraction = Devastation.

Xanatos! Granta Omega's father had devised that formula for orchestrating evil to take root. He had done it at the Jedi Temple itself, hoping to destroy it forever. Could it be that his son was using the same formula to destroy the Senate? Was that his real goal?

If Omega was behind this Senatorial effort, he had already succeeded in disrupting the Senate, demoralizing the Jedi, and distracting everyone. But if that was truly the case, what was the coming devastation he was planning?

Obi-Wan didn't know. But suddenly he knew in his bones that his earlier instinct was dead-on. Omega was behind this.

". . . and I'm sorry to be the one to tell you this," Tyro was saying, "but it was inevitable given the circumstances, I suppose."

Obi-Wan wrenched his attention back to his friend. "What is it?"

"Bog Divinian's committee has taken an unusual step. Instead of a recommendation, it has just entered an official petition to ban the Jedi Order from any Senate action. This was clever . . . but not clever enough. Senator Organa found a clause that allowed him to appeal directly to the Chancellor in a separate closed-door session. Palpatine is scheduled to decide on the matter later this afternoon in a meeting with both Senators."

"This has all just happened since the hearing? I thought the Senate was supposed to be *slow.*"

"Only when real things are getting done," Tyro said drily. "When it comes to political maneuvering, you have to move fast." Tyro gave him a keen look. "What is it, my friend? The Jedi Order is in trouble, but we will find a way to fight, I promise you. You have more friends than enemies. You just have to remind your friends that they are your friends. It's the Senate way."

"The Senate way," Obi-Wan pronounced in disgust. "And what is that? Talk. Deals. Bribes. Corruption."

"Obi-Wan." Tyro silenced him gently. "I agree with you. All this is true. But I still believe in the Senate. It is the living symbol of the Republic. Until it was formed, the galaxy boiled with chaos. It is our only chance to bring peace to the thousands of worlds that cannot manage alone. There are good beings in the Senate, like Senator Organa. Many of them. They will win in the end."

Obi-Wan had never heard Tyro defend the Senate so passionately before. Usually, he railed against it. But of course that was why he continued to toil down in his little office, searching for ways to make it better. "What amazes me is that you keep your faith in the Senate, no matter how many times your heart is broken."

"Oh, my heart may break from time to time, but never my will," Tyro said lightly. "In that way we are alike. Now, tell me what worries you."

"It's not so much the petition, but what the petition might conceal," Obi-Wan explained.

Tyro shook his head. "I don't understand."

"What if this action to discredit the Jedi is just a diversion so that something worse could occur?" Obi-Wan said.

What he liked about Tyro was that his friend did not waste time. His small, furred face grew intent. "Ah. Of course. Continue."

"I have been tracking Granta Omega and Jenna Zan Arbor, both of whom are familiar to you," Obi-Wan said to Tyro's nod. "What if they were behind this latest scheme? What if it is merely a smokescreen for their real plan?"

The possibilities clicked through Tyro's brain. "Of course if it is true that they're involved, this would be more than possible — it would be likely," he said rapidly. "It fits with the way Omega operates. And it makes sense, since Sano Sauro is involved." Tyro's face contracted into an expression of distaste. Sauro was his enemy, too. "That would explain why he has remained in the background. He doesn't want us to connect him to this campaign, because he knows we will immediately make the connection to Omega."

"There is something we're not seeing here," Obi-Wan said.

"The Chancellor is, of course, a big supporter of the Jedi," Tyro said, thinking. "It's unlikely that he will approve the petition. Bog and Sauro could then manipulate this defeat into a call for a no-confidence vote. That would allow them to propose Sauro as Chancellor. I know that is his ultimate ambition."

"Then Omega would control the Senate," Obi-Wan said slowly.

Tyro tapped his tapered fingers on the manuals. "But Palpatine is too powerful and too skilled to be out-maneuvered. And I doubt even Sauro could muster enough support for a vote of no confidence. Let's see, he controls the Viga alliance, and the planets in the Commerce Guild, and . . . yes, he could get several systems in the Mid-Rim. But in the Core? No. He's powerful, but he's actively disliked, and there is a strong opposition faction headed by Bail Organa that can't be discounted."

Tyro ended his speculation, realizing that Obi-Wan had grown impatient with the details of Senate politics.

"In conclusion," he said, sighing, "I have no conclusion. I can't see them trying such a thing. You don't try something like that unless you're sure you can succeed. Palpatine is tremendously popular, especially at the moment. Tomorrow there will be a ceremony for the opening of the All Planets Relief Fund. A huge group of supporters will be attending—including many Jedi. This is Palpatine's pet project, and it's a good one. He's worked his way through the tangled bureaucracy to get it off the ground. Now any world in peril can petition the Senate directly for funds through one central account. Palpatine claims this will stop the bureaucratic slowdown for relief to troubled worlds. You see, before this, a world would have to petition the committee for Relief, which would then turn the matter over to a specially appointed investigatory committee, which would then —"

Obi-Wan's comlink signaled, and he held up a hand to interrupt Tyro. He had to admit he was relieved not to get a crash course in the now outdated procedural details of Senate relief efforts.

Siri's crisp voice came through the comlink. "We found something. Possibly Omega and Zan Arbor's hideout. We need backup. They could be inside."

She gave him the coordinates. Obi-Wan stood as he flipped his comlink closed and put it back in his belt — at last, action and not meetings. "I have to go."

"And you will take care, I hope. I think you are right.

Our enemies are hidden, and that makes them more dangerous." Tyro held his hand out, fingers spread. Obi-Wan pressed his own spread-fingered palm against it. It was the gesture of good-bye that the Svivreni made to only those closest to them.

The Svivreni did not say good-bye. They considered it bad luck.

"So go," Tyro said in the Svivreni farewell.

CHAPTER TEN

Obi-Wan was well acquainted with the many exit doors of the Senate complex, and he hit the streets of Coruscant in minutes. He took a vertical monorail down a hundred stories to the business district where Siri and Ferus were located, near the bank of Aargau. On the way, he contacted Anakin.

As he rounded the last corner he saw his apprentice streaking down through the air. Looking up, Obi-Wan could see that Anakin had made the jump from a platform twenty stories up.

"I'm sure there was a lift tube," Obi-Wan said as Anakin ran up. "Or even stairs."

Anakin grinned. "Too slow."

Together, they ran up to Siri and Ferus, who had taken up a position behind a jumble of airspeeders parked in front of an interior mall of popular shops and restaurants.

"We got a tip from an informer," Siri said. She pointed to a small white building across the way. A blinking sign said VIRTUAL HAPPINESS. Another sign, smaller and clumsily handwritten said: OUT OF BUSINESS.

"It was one of those sim-voyage places," Siri said. "You know, where you can go and have a simulated vacation experience to the luxury worlds of the Core. But our source says a couple moved in a few days ago. They said they were starting a business, but nothing has been done, and they only exit the building at night."

"It could be anyone," Obi-Wan said.

"Ferus did a quick check of the airspeeders parked here," Siri said, with a look that told Obi-Wan he should wait for her to finish. "Nothing unusual came up. Then he did a check with Coruscant security and went through the tickets for illegally parked airspeeders, cross-checking with known IDs used by the Slams. A standard Ralion B-14 that was recently bought at a speeder lot twenty levels down matched one of the false ID docs the Slams had on their master ship."

"Good work," Obi-Wan said to Ferus. "I say we go in. We don't have time to waste."

They strode to the door. As soon as they did, a buzzer sounded, and a light flashed. An automated female voice said in a pleasant tone, "Welcome. We're not home. If you wish to leave a text message, use the keypad."

"I have a message, all right," Obi-Wan said, drawing his lightsaber. "We're coming in."

He plunged his lightsaber through the door. It disintegrated from the center out.

The house was dark inside. Obi-Wan stepped in.

Immediately, lights blazed. Sound blared. He heard the sound of rockets, and he fell to the ground and rolled, lightsaber ready to deflect. Behind him, the Jedi moved in to flank him.

The walls flickered and pulsed with sound and light. It took a few seconds for Obi-Wan to make sense of it, then he realized every wall held a moving image, a holo-projection of a separate scene. One was a field with exploding novas in the sky — the famous shooting stars of Nantama. Another was of the mountains of Belazura. Another showed fireworks exploding over the translucent seas of Dremulae. All were popular vacationing spots.

The noise was at full volume — surf, fireworks, wind. So loud that at first he didn't hear the *whirr* of the seeker droids.

He was leaping before the others, cutting down two in a perfect swoop of the lightsaber. The droids peppered the walls with blaster fire. Smoke rose and the noise was deafening. The images flickered in beautiful colors of blue and rose and green while the shadows of the droids moved in menacing circles. The electric *ping* of the blaster fire crisscrossed the space, and each Jedi had to jump, whirl, and slash at the droids as they dived and circled.

Within minutes, the dozen or so droids were reduced to smoking scrap on the floor. Obi-Wan strode over to a panel behind the door and shut down the holoprojection system.

"Careful, that might be —" Siri started, as a secret blast door opened and three combat droids, the deadly droidekas, wheeled out and clattered to life. Blazing blasterfire raked the area where Obi-Wan had stood. Anyone but a Jedi would have been instantly annihilated.

"Booby-trapped!" Siri yelled, as she dodged the blaster bolts.

With deflector shields in place, droidekas were difficult to stop. While the rest of the Jedi took a step backward, Anakin moved forward. He had studied the droids ever since learning about them, and knew the precise spot where their generators lay. He rolled onto the floor, for only an upward stroke could disable them.

The Force hummed in the room as Anakin deftly inserted his lightsaber once, twice, three times. The roar of blasters ended.

Now the floor was littered with droids. Other than that, the house was empty.

"Let's search," Obi-Wan said. "They might have left a clue."

Siri moved past a table. "The only thing they left was dirty dishes," she said, disdainfully pointing to several greasy plates on the table.

Other than the signs of a hastily abandoned meal, there wasn't a trace of the occupants to be found.

"We've come up empty again," Siri said in disgust after a few minutes of searching.

"It's Omega's style," Anakin said. "He knows how to leave without a trace."

Ferus nudged a half-open closet door with his foot. "Nothing."

Obi-Wan drifted to the table. He bent over the dishes. There was a scrap of roll on one plate, and a puddle of sauce on the other. He bent closer and sniffed.

"Gotcha," he murmured.

"What is it, Master?" Anakin asked, turning.

Obi-Wan pointed to the plate. "That's Dexter Jettster's slider garnish. I'd know it anywhere."

Siri strode over and looked at the plate. "Congratulations. Our best clue is a garnish."

"It's a place to start," Obi-Wan said.

Siri nodded. "Why don't you and Anakin head over to Dexter's Diner and ask some questions. I think Ferus and I should study the water delivery system here on Coruscant. We know they're here. We'd better have a good idea of what damage they could do."

"Good idea. We'll be in touch."

Obi-Wan signaled to Anakin, and they left the house. Dexter's Diner wasn't far, lying in nearby Coco Town. They hurried through the crowded pedestrian ramps. The monorails were packed, and it was faster to walk.

They crossed through the plaza on the way to the diner. The buildings ringing the plaza were a mix of low-rent business and dilapidated industrial warehouses. Dexter's Diner crouched between the bigger buildings, its bright sign casting a red glow through the gray day.

Anakin started toward the door, but Obi-Wan stopped him. "Wait. Look who's inside."

Anakin peered into the window. Sitting alone in a booth, both hands cupping a mug, was Astri.

CHAPTER ELEVEN

Astri looked up, surprised, when Obi-Wan and Anakin slid into her booth. She had been so lost in thought that she hadn't seen them enter the diner.

"It's funny to see you here," she said to Obi-Wan. "Like a dream. I was just thinking of the old days. Everything is so different now. Even here." She looked around. "Dexter actually made it into a profitable enterprise."

"Well, he doesn't give away meals and drinks the way Didi did," Obi-Wan said.

She smiled. "That's true." She held up her empty cup. "He doesn't even give refills. But I like it here."

"Yes, those *were* good days," Obi-Wan said. "Things *are* more complicated now. Like the fact that your husband is trying to destroy the Jedi Order."

Astri's hands tightened on her cup. "I long ago made it a policy not to discuss Bog's politics."

"So what do you think about, then?" Anakin asked. His question wasn't confrontational. It was easy, interested. Obi-Wan was relieved that his Padawan had interfered so gracefully. He realized that he was deeply angry with Astri. He had expected better of her.

No expectations. Acceptance.

It was the Jedi way. And sometimes, so very hard to follow.

"My relief work," Astri responded promptly. "The economy of my adopted world, Nuralee, is failing."

"I didn't know that," Obi-Wan said. "The last time I was on Nuralee it was prospering."

She looked down into her empty cup. "That was probably some time ago."

Before Bog took office, Obi-Wan guessed.

"There are many too poor to buy food. I'm here on Coruscant briefly, just to attend a meeting to ask for help from the new All Planets Relief Fund and attend the inaugural ceremony. A Jedi team is acting as couriers and protectors for a shipment of food and medical supplies to Nuralee, and I must return to ensure it gets in the right hands."

"Do you know who they are?" Anakin asked.

"Soara Antana and Darra Thel-Tanis," Astri said. "I am grateful for their help."

You are grateful for the help we give you, but you will not help us. Obi-Wan had the thought but would not say it aloud.

No expectations. Just acceptance.

And as he thought the words, his mind cleared. Now that he was sitting quietly with her, he allowed himself to truly look at her, not just her changed hair and clothes, but what her face revealed. Yes, she was distant and remote. But if he removed his own feelings from the situation, he could see more clearly.

Something was wrong. He was picking up something.

Fear. She was afraid. But of what?

"So you are returning soon," Anakin said.

"The day after tomorrow. I am anxious to see my son and Didi."

Obi-Wan leaned back, still studying Astri without seeming to. She looked away, twining her fingers through the handle of her cup.

"So has Bog seen what Dex has done to the old place?" Anakin asked in a jovial tone, gesturing toward the red stools and the curved counter.

Excellent, Anakin. A casual question, but it would

give them the information they needed to know. Was there a connection between Bog and the safe house?

"Yes, he's been here." Astri pushed away her empty cup. The subject of her husband didn't interest her. But they had the answer they wanted.

Bog had been the one to bring food from Dex's Diner to Omega and the others. There was a link between them now. Not a link he could prove. But a link.

Astri began to slide out of the booth. "I should go. I'm late. It's always good to see you, Obi-Wan. Anakin."

She hurried out the door, not waiting for their good-byes. As she left, she almost collided with a cloaked figure who was also leaving.

Obi-Wan stared after her. Even the way she moved was different. He remembered Astri striding down the streets, her curls flying, her face uptilted, her eyes alight, taking everything in. Now she walked with her head down, her hands thrust into the deep pockets of her tunic.

"She's afraid," he said out loud.

"Yes," Anakin said. "But not for herself. For her son."

Obi-Wan wrenched his gaze from the departing Astri and looked at his Padawan. More and more, he was recognizing that Anakin's sensitivity to others was growing and surpassing his in some cases. Anakin often seemed to know what secrets were inside others, what drove them to do the puzzling things they did. It had something to do with his command of the Force, but it was more than that.

He remembered the words of Ferus, when he had confessed his doubts about Anakin to Obi-Wan on Romln. He had said that Anakin wanted to control everything. Anakin's gift of seeing inside beings could turn dangerous if he tried to control the feelings he found instead of just observing them.

But that was a Jedi lesson ingrained in every Padawan. Anakin knew that.

"Master, I have to ask you something," he said now. "Supreme Chancellor Palpatine has offered me a chance to observe the proceedings he attends over the next few days. He thinks I would gain insight into the political arena of the Senate."

"I agree," Obi-Wan said. "I have no objections, as long as it doesn't interfere with our pursuit of Omega. You could learn something valuable that could help us. It is a great honor that Palpatine has bestowed on you, my young Padawan."

Dexter waddled out from behind the counter, wiping his four hands on his greasy apron.

"Obi-Wan! My friend! Why didn't you come back to the kitchen and greet me?" Dexter's wide face creased in an enormous grin. "And you brought the tadpole with you!"

Anakin winced at the nickname. Then he stood up. He had grown since the last time Dexter had seen him, and Dexter burst out with a shout of laughter.

"Well, you showed me, you did, young Skywalker. I'd say you were full-grown now!" He hooked one enormous foot over a chair rail and dragged it over to the booth, then eased his bulk onto it.

"Now, what can I get the two of you — ten-alarm chili? Sliders? I've got a stew cooking with bantha meat, cooked long and slow to make it tender. I know they say banthas taste like old boots, but they haven't tasted Dex's stew! I'll tell you my secret, boys." Dex leaned over. "I leave the hooves in the pot while it's cooking."

"Sounds delicious, Dex, but we've come for information," Obi-Wan said quickly, as Anakin's face paled. "We're on the trail of some galactic criminals, and we believe they have a taste for your slider garnish."

Dex slapped his knees with two of his hands. "And who doesn't? I've got to remember to bottle it. I could make my fortune! One of these days, when I get a minute away from the stove, ha!"

"One of the criminals is Jenna Zan Arbor."

Dex whistled. "A nasty piece of work. Wouldn't know her to see her, though. And I haven't heard she's back on Coruscant."

"How about Senator Bog Divinian?"

"Astri Oddo's husband? Sure, he's been here. Likes my sliders. You know, some people find them addictive! Picks up his dinner many a time and brings it back to his lodgings."

Obi-Wan briefly described the Slams. "Have you seen them?"

Dex stroked his chin. "Don't think so, and haven't heard of them, either. Hard to say. Here's the problem — we've been too busy here lately to notice much of anything except dirty dishes. And things are set to get even busier tomorrow, because the All Planets Relief Fund Ceremony will be held right across the way." With one fat finger, Dex pointed out the window to the plaza. "This is the kind of area the Fund will be trying to improve. Anyway, I'll keep my eye out. Many will be coming to see the big shots like the Chancellor. But most will come, I'd wager, to see a fortune being transferred. Everyone likes to be close to vertex, even if they don't have any themselves. They feel richer for looking at it — at least until they go home and look around at what they've got!" Dex laughed heartily.

Anakin looked at Obi-Wan. Fortune? Vertex? "What do you mean, Dex?" he asked.

"Don't you know the drill? Every planet in the Senate is donating vertex to the new fund. They present it to Palpatine, and then his personal guard brings it to the vault." Dex pointed across the plaza. "The Bank of the Core. Now don't be thinking there will be hanky-panky," he said, waggling his finger. "There will be security like you've never seen. Coruscant security and the Chancellor's Red Guards. Tomorrow they'll be cordoning off walkways and placing officers around the plaza. A journalist for the HoloNet news even paid me to keep her airspeeder out back so she'd be able to take off quick tomorrow to get to her vidcam studio hookup. I said yes because she was a looker — or maybe it was the credits she put in my hand, ha! Then she goes and parks it so it blocks my food-delivery doors. Left it locked tight as a drum. Now you know I don't stand for that." Dex chuckled. "So I got my pal Acey to break in and I moved it myself behind a dumpster."

Dex's words washed over Obi-Wan. There was something here. Item after item clicked in, but he couldn't add them up.

"Can we see that airspeeder, Dex?"

Dex gave him a puzzled look. "Don't see why, but what I have is yours, Obi-Wan. This way."

CHAPTER TWELVE

Anakin and Obi-Wan followed Dex through the steamy kitchen noisy with clattering pans and spattering grease, through the rear exit doors into the alley. A long airspeeder was parked in an angle, wedged between a dumpster and durasteel trash bins.

"It'll smell like old fish tomorrow, but I can't help it. They can't block my kitchen," Dexter said.

"It's a Ralion B-14." Anakin said.

"Can you show me how it was parked before you moved it, Dex?" Obi-Wan asked.

Dexter stamped his enormous foot. "Right here. In the way."

Obi-Wan bent over and studied a round cover sunk into the duracrete street. He knocked on it with his knuckles. "Utility tunnel."

"For my water delivery," Dexter said. "I know because my water froze last winter, and that's where they crawled down to fix it."

Anakin and Obi-Wan exchanged a glance. It was all adding up.

"Got to check on my stew. You two come in when you have more time. You know I like to feed you." Dexter waddled back into the diner.

"Must have been Valadon in disguise," Obi-Wan said. "The airspeeder is for their getaway. And here," he said, stamping his foot on the cover, "is one of the entrance points for the Zone, most likely."

Anakin prowled around the airspeeder. "Doesn't seem to be juiced up, at least on the outside. No extra exhaust valves. Seats four, five in a crunch." He opened the door and slid inside.

Obi-Wan entered the speeder from the other end. "Looks clean."

"Fully fueled," Anakin noted.

Obi-Wan reached over toward the door on his side. Something had drifted down to the floor when he'd opened the door, the tiniest wisp of a thing. Attuned to notice every scrap, he bent over to pick it up. It was a thread. He held it up. Blue.

"Anything?" Anakin asked.

"I'll send it to the Temple lab for analysis, but it

looks like standard cloth," Obi-Wan said, carefully placing it in his utility belt. "Certainly not the septsilk and veda cloth that both Zan Arbor and the Slams like to wear."

Anakin murmured a reply, busy studying the engine specs. "This doesn't make sense," he said. "The transport body style doesn't fit the engine. In speeders, you maximize every particle of space. I'd guess there is about three centimeters unaccounted for."

"That's not very much."

"Oh, yes it is." Anakin looked over at his Master. "It's just like the Slams' ship. They knew how to hide secret compartments in tiny spaces."

Anakin was already reaching under the dash. Obi-Wan felt along the floor and the edges of his seat. He had found a few compartments on the Slams' ship, but Anakin had found all of them.

"Got it." A drawer popped out toward Anakin. He reached inside, then tossed an item to Obi-Wan.

Obi-Wan examined the palm-sized datapad. He switched it on. "It's a map of the plaza," Obi-Wan said as he accessed the file. "With notations on street closings and space lanes." Obi-Wan pressed a few more indicators. "And the water transport tunnels are marked."

"Omega, Zan Arbor, and the Slams are planning to heist the new Relief Fund treasury," Anakin said.

"That's what they're after. Not only will it give them a fortune to operate with, it will embarrass Palpatine."

"It will be a political victory as well as a personal one. That's most likely why Bog and Sauro got involved — they are looking at a way to strike a blow against Palpatine. And if they profit from it as well, why not?"

"With the help of the Zone, a small band like the Slams can get around the entire Coruscant security force," Anakin said, shaking his head.

Obi-Wan nodded. "And in his arrogance, Omega expects to defeat the Jedi, too. If the Jedi Order allows the heist to happen, they will be disgraced. That will help Bog and Sauro pass their petition — or win a no-confidence vote against the Chancellor."

His eyes gleamed at Anakin, and Anakin caught the spark. He felt a spurt of excitement. The pieces were falling into place.

"At last we are one step ahead of Omega," Obi-Wan said. "Now all we have to do is set the trap."

CHAPTER THIRTEEN

Anakin expected his Master to explode into movement. Obi-Wan never wasted time. Instead, Obi-Wan just looked at him.

"So?"

"So?" Anakin asked cautiously.

"What next?"

"You want me to decide?"

Obi-Wan nodded. "When you become a Jedi Knight, you'll have to strategize as well as act."

There were a number of things to be done, and at first, they crowded Anakin's brain so that he wasn't sure which to do first. But then a moment later everything was clear and he knew what to do.

"First, we should contact Siri and Ferus and tell them what we know, so that they can concentrate their study of the water system on the area around the plaza," Anakin said. "Then, we should contact Master Windu. The Jedi Council needs to come up with its own plans to protect the vertex during the ceremony."

"Good."

"And we should request a meeting with Chancellor Palpatine," Anakin went on. "It's the only way we can get across the seriousness of what we think is going to happen. After all, it's just guesswork, and it could be easily dismissed. But we should be able to convince him to increase security and put monitors on the water systems. Though . . ." Anakin tapped his fingers on the dashboard ". . . if we do nothing and simply allow them to sabotage the system with the Zone, we have an advantage."

Obi-Wan frowned. "We do?"

"The Jedi will not be affected, but our enemy won't know that. Omega and the Slams will be lulled into the belief that they have succeeded. In other words, we give them what they want in the beginning. But we control the outcome."

"But Anakin, that means exposing thousands of beings to the Zone."

"It's not toxic. The beings will have an extraordinarily pleasant morning, that's all."

Obi-Wan's frown grew deeper. "We don't know that.

You experienced it early on. We don't know what Zan Arbor has done to it since then. Are you forgetting the four workers who died?"

"But we have every reason to believe the system has been perfected." Anakin hesitated. He could see that he had displeased his Master. "But of course we don't know that for sure. So we must guard the entry ports to the system so the Zone cannot be deployed."

Obi-Wan nodded. "Anything else?"

Anakin thought briefly. "No. Not at the moment."

"I agree. Let's go."

They headed for the Senate. While Obi-Wan called ahead to request a meeting with Chancellor Palpatine, Anakin brooded on his mistake. He had seen the uneasiness in his Master's eyes, though it had passed quickly. Sometimes he made mistakes and wasn't sure why they were wrong. He knew that his Master's deepest desire was to capture Omega. Anakin wondered how much it was permissible to risk in order to accomplish that. How much risk was too much? Who was best to judge? He wished he could ask Obi-Wan those questions, but he didn't want to displease him further.

As soon as they arrived at the Chancellor's office, they were ushered in to see him. He stood at the large window behind his desk, ready to receive them.

"Sly Moore tells me this is urgent," he said. "She is

not accustomed to such vehemence. I hope it's not bad news."

"Well, that depends," Obi-Wan said. Quickly, he filled Palpatine in on what they had discovered and what they suspected.

"Naturally," Obi-Wan concluded, "the best thing to do is to cancel the ceremony."

"I think not," Palpatine said. "This fund has been the result of years of steady work on the part of many worlds. It is a tribute to the very ideals the Galactic Senate was founded upon originally — cooperation and benevolence. I hardly think that canceling the ceremony would help us in any way."

Anakin wasn't surprised, and neither was Obi-Wan.

"Then security must be increased," Obi-Wan said.

"I assure you, the best measures are already in place," Palpatine said. "And I have every confidence in the Jedi's abilities to forestall these villains."

"Then the water system should be shut off in that quadrant."

"And disrupt thousands of lives?" Palpatine looked impatient. "We will monitor the system, of course. Place guards on the entry points. That won't be diffi-cult. If we know there will be an attempt, we will be able to foil it. Now, I have the distasteful task of having to attend a procedural hearing with Senator Divinian."

Palpatine directed his gaze at Obi-Wan. "May I borrow your apprentice? I think it could be a valuable experience for him."

Obi-Wan nodded. "I'll return to the Temple and talk to Master Windu and Siri," he told Anakin. "Keep in contact."

Anakin watched Obi-Wan stride out of the office. He would rather be leaving with him, but he had asked to be included in the Chancellor's meetings, so he had to go.

"Capturing this Omega is important to your Master," Palpatine remarked as they left the office and started down the hall.

"It's important to the galaxy," Anakin said. "He's a dangerous enemy."

"Yes, but not the *most* dangerous enemy," Palpatine said. "From my experience, the most dangerous enemy is the one you can't see."

They drew up in front of a hearing room and walked inside. It was small and private. A long table took up most of the room, with seats equipped with repulsorlift motors that could adjust to the differing heights of many species. Bog sat in a seat at the center of the long table, with Bail Organa opposite him.

Bog spoke into his data recorder in a low tone. "Supreme Chancellor arrived. Meeting will start on time."

Chancellor Palpatine sat at the head of the table and indicated that Anakin take a seat behind him. Bog half-rose, then sat again, as if uncertain what protocol to follow.

"I am here as the head of the Senate investigating committee on Jedi Order abuses," Bog began. "The committee has entered its findings and has delivered an official petition to ban the Jedi from future Senate business. We request from the Supreme Chancellor an override of Senator Organa's counter-petition to stall our petition in a separate committee. We believe it must be debated in the full Senate and acted upon immediately."

Palpatine turned. "Senator Organa?"

"Senators from two hundred planets have signed a protest and request to investigate the petition committee for undue bias in its deliberations," Organa said. "Until that investigation is concluded, the Senate can hardly debate the recommendations of the committee. Let alone vote on the issue."

"I have reached a ruling," Palpatine said.

Bog and Organa looked surprised.

"Th-the Supreme Chancellor has hardly had enough time to consider . . . I have not had a chance to refute . . ." Bog stammered in confusion.

Palpatine held up a hand. "Relax, Senator Divinian.

I rule that you may enter, debate, and vote on the petition to bar the Jedi Order from any further action on behalf of the Galactic Senate."

Palpatine rose, as Bog looked pleased and Bail Organa looked stunned.

"The vote should take place quickly —" Bog urged.

"I agree. The debate and vote shall take place tomorrow after the All Planets Relief Fund ceremony."

Bog stood and bowed. "Thank you for your ruling, Supreme Chancellor. I assure you it is in the best interests of the Senate."

"I assure you that the best interests of the Senate are always my first concern," Palpatine replied, and swept out.

Anakin followed him hastily. He was surprised and dismayed by the meeting. He had expected to hear a spirited debate, and hoped to see the justly renowned Bail Organa in action. But he never expected that Palpatine would rule for Bog.

"You look lost, Anakin," Palpatine said with a slight smile as Anakin swung into step beside him.

"Well, I have to admit I'm surprised. Why did you allow Bog to win?"

"I gave Bog what he wanted because I am sure he will fail," Palpatine replied.

Anakin was suddenly struck. Wasn't this what he

had suggested to Obi-Wan earlier? He had wanted to do the same for their enemy, Omega.

"Bog doesn't know it, but he just destroyed his career," Palpatine said.

Palpatine wasn't gloating, Anakin thought. That would be beneath him. But he did look rather . . . satisfied.

He remembered back on Romin, when he had felt a surge of power, realizing that the Force could not only allow him to move objects, but also to see into motivations and consequences. Many beings were transparent in their greed and ego, just as Bog was. Thinking several steps ahead was not that difficult.

Palpatine understood this; did his Master? Obi-Wan was so cautious. Anakin glanced at Palpatine, admiring how he moved through the Senate halls. He did not exaggerate his power but he did not diminish it. He accepted it and accepted the ways in which he would have to use it.

How satisfying it must feel to simply wait for events to unfold as you have foreseen them, Anakin thought. *How powerful to know the outcome before it happened.* This was what he could learn — and not from his Master. From Palpatine.

CHAPTER FOURTEEN

At the Jedi Temple, Obi-Wan pored over the schematics for the water delivery system in the targeted area of Coruscant. Siri and Ferus showed him what they'd learned from the experts they'd consulted.

The laser map was holoprojected, and Siri used a laser pointer as she spoke. "The access points are here, here, and here, including the tunnel outside Dexter's Diner. They're the most likely places to strike. But of course with Omega we have to think of the least likely, too. That would be here and here. We've got Senate security forces on each point. All undercover, highest-level clearance. In addition, we have Jedi teams patrolling."

Obi-Wan nodded. "Looks good."

"What about the thread analysis?" Ferus asked.

"Looks like a dead end," Obi-Wan reported. "A question of too much information rather than too little. The droid analyst says it's common throughout the galaxy. Thousands of uses and manufacturers. The computers are breaking them down into zones of probability, but . . ."

Siri looked back at the holoprojection map. "We have everything covered, Obi-Wan."

"But you do not feel secure."

Siri's eyebrows knit together. "No."

"Nor do I."

Ferus hooked his fingers into his utility belt. "I have a feeling none of us will be sleeping tonight."

Obi-Wan and Anakin spent the night patrolling the streets and sky lanes. Keeping out of sight, the Jedi made sure the water delivery system remained untouched. Master Windu had allocated the necessary resources to do so. Nevertheless, Anakin and Obi-Wan watched the watchers. They did not know when Omega's team would strike, but they felt they could not trust anyone else to be fully prepared. They knew Omega's cunning.

The first rays of the sun were flashing on the Temple

spires as Obi-Wan and Anakin returned from their rounds. Waiting for them in the Great Hall were Jedi Master Soara Antana and her apprentice, Darra Haariden.

Anakin hurried forward to greet his friend Darra. He had barely seen her since their mission to Norah, where she'd been wounded.

"How are you doing?" he asked.

"Running on a full tank," she replied, her eyes smiling.

Meanwhile, Obi-Wan drew Soara aside.

"Thank you for coming so quickly," he said. "Is everything . . ."

Soara nodded. "They're having breakfast at the moment. Master Alann is with them."

Anakin overheard and shot his Master a curious look, but Obi-Wan merely said, "Meet us at Dexter's Diner at the prearranged time."

Anakin joined Obi-Wan. He raised his eyebrows in a question.

"The fear you saw on Astri's face," Obi-Wan said grimly. "I want to make it go away."

It took some persuading, but Astri agreed to meet him. Obi-Wan waited outside Dexter's Diner. When he saw her approach, he walked forward to greet her.

"Obi-Wan, I can't interfere with Bog, even for you,"

she said before he could speak. "I'm a Senator's wife now."

"Why can't you meet my eyes, Astri?" he asked.

"Don't be ridiculous," she said, but her gaze kept moving.

"Are you afraid you were followed?"

"No. I took precautions." Astri saw her mistake. She bit her lip.

"You are afraid," Obi-Wan said. "Don't worry, you weren't followed. There are Jedi watching your every move now. And yet you still can't meet my eyes."

All he could see was the top of her head. The dark curls that once tumbled down her back were now cropped close against her skull. He remembered when she had shaved off her hair in order to impersonate a bounty hunter. Astri had never had much vanity. She was a pure spirit, and he had misjudged her.

"I am ashamed," she said quietly. "That is why I can't meet your eyes."

He took her arm and led her into the shelter of the diner overhang. "There is no need for shame, old friend," he said softly. "We have been through worse together."

She shook her head. "No. We have not." She looked up, and he saw that her deep green eyes glistened with tears. "Now I have a child."

"And Bog has threatened him."

"He will take him away. He is so young, Obi-Wan. I cannot let that happen. No matter what. Even your friendship, even the entire Jedi Order is nothing to me in the face of that. I know that making a choice for one life against so many lives is wrong, but I cannot help myself." This time, she did not drop her eyes.

"Astri, that is not a cause for shame. I understand it. Of course that is what you must do."

"You understand that I couldn't help you?"

Obi-Wan nodded. "And you must understand that I must help *you*."

"There is no help for me. Even from the Jedi."

"Look." He took her by the shoulders and spun her around. Now she could see inside the diner. Her father, Didi, was comparing recipes with Dexter. Lune, her son, was sitting on a stool, swinging his legs as Darra teased him, making him laugh. A large plate of Dex's special cakes sat in front of the child. He picked up a piece with his fingers and ate it, then licked his fingers.

Astri put a hand on her heart.

"I had Soara and Darra bring them. We can arrange to have them back before anyone knows they are missing, if that is your choice. But there is another."

Astri waited, her eyes drinking in the sight of her son.

"You can leave Bog. The Jedi will offer you protection."

She was already shaking her head. "He will find me. He will win." She turned. "You don't understand, Obi-Wan. He's not as stupid as he appears. He is cunning. I didn't realize . . . I didn't know . . . the lengths he would go. He got one taste of power, and it corrupted him. He has aligned himself with the worst in the galaxy. It started so softly. A favor for the Commerce Guild. Then another. And soon he was approached by another Senator —"

"Sano Sauro."

"Yes. He sold his honor. Well, the honor I thought he had. And now there is someone else, someone so powerful he does not say his name."

"Granta Omega. And with Omega, Jenna Zan Arbor. Did you know that?"

Astri looked away. "Yes. I knew that. And still I did nothing."

He slipped his hand into her cold one and squeezed it briefly. "You were alone. Now you are not. You still have me."

"Bog was never a strong man," she said. "How strange it is to fear him now."

She reached into the pocket of her tunic and handed several disks to Obi-Wan.

"What is this?"

"Bog's data recorder. For his memoirs." She made a face. "I copied them secretly. He says it only keeps a record of meetings, but that's not true. He is too vain to hide what he thinks of as his accomplishments. There might be something on these."

Obi-Wan slipped them into his tunic. "You didn't know I had brought Lune and Didi here. Why did you bring the disks?"

"I've been carrying them with me. Seeing you, I felt so guilty, going along with Bog. I thought, there must be a way to help somehow. Bog is involved in something terrible. It is more than scheming against the Jedi in the Senate. There is some kind of plot, a takeover that will net him more power. He can't resist boasting to me. Soon we'll be able to afford whatever we want. A luxury cruiser for our trips to Nuralee. A villa by the Sea of Translucency on Dremulae."

"Dremulae?"

"Yes, he saw an image of the perfect spot, he said."

Yes, Obi-Wan thought, *in Omega's safe house.*

"He has these grand plans. And he's questioned me closely about the details of what will take place during the Relief Fund ceremony. I was on the planning committee. I can't imagine what that means."

"I can," Obi-Wan said. "Astri, I promise you, after today you will not have to worry about Bog Divinian."

She looked up into his face. Something came over her, some jolt of courage or certainty, and she nodded. "Thank you, old friend."

"And now," Obi-Wan said in a lighter tone, "it is time to greet your son. I think he's almost out of cakes."

CHAPTER FIFTEEN

Everything was in place. Secret security milled in the crowd. There were infrared sensors on the gravsled with the treasury. Extra guards in the Core Bank itself. Droids buzzed overhead as thick as flies.

Obi-Wan stood to the side. In his ear was an earpiece in which Bog Divinian's voice droned on. Bog's recordings were filled with the dullest details, from when he took a tea break to the compliment paid him by the visiting ruler of Teevan. Obi-Wan noted that he even planned how late to be for the Senate hearing on the anti-Jedi petition. Six minutes. Short enough so that no one would be offended, long enough to demonstrate his importance, Obi-Wan guessed.

None of the information was useful, and none of it was valuable, including Bog's insights into Senate politics. Still, Obi-Wan continued to listen. He had given a copy to Tyro, but he wanted to hear for himself.

The speeches on the platform were only slightly more interesting. One Senator after another came up and thanked the others and Palpatine, even while managing to convey that it was through his or her own early support that the idea really took off.

In his ear, Bog worked on a speech. Obi-Wan could even hear his footsteps as he paced.

In this time of great grief and sorrow . . .

No. In this perilous time, we look to a leader who can take us from strong to stronger . . .

No, that's not quite the tone. More . . . leaderlike.

Now only one of us can lead us through the valley of fear to the mountaintop of solidarity . . .

Obi-Wan switched off the recorder. Chancellor Palpatine was speaking, which meant the ceremony was almost over.

"I accept this treasury on behalf of the Senate, and thank all the generous worlds that contributed," Palpatine said, with one hand on the armored repulsorlift wagon that held the glittering gold boxes of vertex. "This is the dawn of a new age. An age where help will arrive when and where it is most needed. Thank you all."

Palpatine, at least, had learned the value of brevity and modesty, Obi-Wan noted.

He watched as the Supreme Chancellor stepped back and entered his personal transport. He sped off toward the Senate. The others Senators followed. There was a debate to attend.

The Blue and Red Guards, Palpatine's personal guards, slowly guided the vehicle to the great open doors of the vault of the Core Bank. Obi-Wan felt a murmur go through the crowd. Dex was right. There was nothing like a huge fortune to cause beings to swoon.

And still there was no sign of trouble. Obi-Wan saw Siri through the crowd. She shrugged. Anakin had his gaze fixed on the vault.

Obi-Wan's comlink signaled. It was Tyro.

"Anything?" Obi-Wan asked.

"That speech he's practicing . . . did you get to that yet? Any impressions?"

"He needs a speechwriter."

"Yes, it's awful, but did you get the subject?"

"No, I couldn't figure out what he was talking about. It didn't make sense."

"That's what worries me."

Obi-Wan watched the Guards move into the building. "So what's your point?"

"Well, what's *his* point, that's the question. Obi-Wan, this may be off-base, but . . ."

Obi-Wan noticed that one of the Blue Guards had a torn hem. Unusual for these guards. They took their position as personal guards to Palpatine seriously.

Torn hem. Blue thread.

"Later, Tyro." Obi-Wan snapped his comlink shut and vaulted through the crowd. Anakin caught his movement.

"The guards!" he bellowed.

And then they were all moving — Anakin, Siri, Ferus, as the durasteel doors began to slide shut on the vault.

Obi-Wan leaped. He slammed against the vault door, then squeezed himself inside, nearly leaving his foot behind as the door clanged shut. Anakin was above him, timing his own leap to slither through the doors as they closed.

Obi-Wan landed on the floor and tackled the Blue Guard in front of him. The helmet was knocked off, and he looked into the face of Roper Slam.

"Not you again!" Slam groaned.

Anakin tackled the next guard. It was Slam's sidekick, Valadon.

"This was supposed to be *easy!*" Slam yelped.

Valadon struggled to release herself from Anakin's grip. "What happened to that Zone? We weren't supposed to meet any resistance!"

"We've been double-crossed," Slam said. He didn't struggle with Obi-Wan. He sat cross-legged on the floor, then tried to rip off the robe in angry frustration.

Siri and Ferus ran in through the interior door of the vault, followed by anxious-looking officials and part of the security force.

"It's all right," Obi-Wan said. "You can take them into custody."

"There wasn't even an attempt to hit the water system," Siri said.

"You see? Double-crossed," Slam said, slumping down.

"Another two minutes and we would have been out of here with the vertex," Valadon said.

"Everything depends on minutes, Val," Slam said. "We live and die on minutes."

Minutes, Obi-Wan thought.

Bog is going to be six minutes late for the debate.

To make himself more important? Or was there another reason?

Now only one of us can lead us through the valley of fear to the mountaintop of solidarity . . .

It doesn't make sense. That's what worries me. . . .

The truth blazed a path inside his brain. Bog was practicing a *nominating* speech. A speech he would deliver sometime today.

The heist was yet another diversion.

The nominating speech was for Sano Sauro to take over as Supreme Chancellor.

The real mission was to assassinate Supreme Chancellor Palpatine.

CHAPTER SIXTEEN

Anakin's head whipped around. One moment Obi-Wan was there, standing over Roper Slam, and the next, he was gone.

Anakin whirled and charged out the door of the vault, into the Core Bank building itself. He was just in time to see his Master racing out the front door.

Anakin put on a burst of speed. Obi-Wan was doing three things at once. He leaped over four chatting security officers straight onto an unattended swoop, even while he slipped his comlink out of his belt and spoke rapidly into it. At the same time, he started the swoop engine.

Anakin jumped onto an empty swoop and revved the engine, lifting into the sky just as a security officer yelled, "Hey!"

Within seconds, he had caught up to his Master.

"What's up?" Anakin asked easily, even though they were going the wrong way down a space lane.

Obi-Wan went into a screeching dive to avoid a crowded airbus. When Anakin caught up, he said, "I think Omega's real goal is to use the Zone at the Senate and assassinate Palpatine. I've already tried to call Senate security, but I can't get through. All of security is caught up in the ceremony."

"Which is probably what he's counting on. We'd better hurry, then." Anakin pushed the speed on his swoop. Obi-Wan did the same.

They looped, dove, and flew flat-out, dipping out of the space lane to do some highly illegal flying over the pedestrian walkways leading to the Senate. Obi-Wan leaped off the swoop as it was still flying and held out a hand, using the Force to guide it to a safe stop. Anakin followed.

They ran into the Senate building, past the enormous statues. As he ran, Obi-Wan contacted Siri and told her what he suspected.

"I'll contact Master Windu and head to the Senate. We'll need backup. The head of security is here, I'll talk to him."

"Do what you can." Obi-Wan shoved his comlink into his belt.

"How do you think they'll do it?" Anakin asked as they ran along the elevated walkway leading to Palpatine's private office.

"They'll use the Zone to impair the opposition Senators. They will have figured out a way to target them somehow, maybe by inviting them to the meeting first. That's why Bog is going to be late. Then they'll call for a vote and oust the Jedi Order. In the meantime, they'll assassinate Palpatine."

"So they will have eliminated Jedi interference and Palpatine in one day," Anakin said.

"And Sano Sauro will be Supreme Chancellor."

They raced into Palpatine's outer office. Sly Moore gazed at them forbiddingly, her pale eyes showing her disapproval. "Not another emergency meeting. The Supreme Chancellor is busy."

"This is life or death," Obi-Wan told her.

She hesitated a fraction of an instant. "He has already gone to the Jedi vote in the Senate. He took the South Corridor!" she shouted after them as they ran.

They raced down the hallways. They couldn't be too late. They couldn't let Omega win.

Ahead they saw Palpatine walking. Obi-Wan skidded up to him and pushed him into an empty meeting room. When he touched his arm, he was shocked at how thin the Supreme Chancellor was. Yet his arm was like a braiding of durasteel, ropy and strong. Something clanged along Obi-Wan's nerves, some feeling, some instinct that made him want to recoil. He felt dread well up in him, and he wondered if he was too late, after all. Perhaps there was something he had not seen. Was he missing something? Obi-Wan felt suddenly confused.

"Master Kenobi, what is it?" Palpatine asked. He had moved his arm away quickly and was now adjusting the high collar on his cloak.

"An assassination plot against you, Supreme Chancellor," Obi-Wan said. "Granta Omega is behind it. I am sure of it. Sano Sauro would be nominated by Bog Divinian as your successor."

Palpatine thought this over. A small smile crossed his thin, bloodless lips. "Of course. That would be the inevitable next step."

"You don't seem very concerned about your potential assassination," Anakin said.

Palpatine waved a hand. "My personal safety ceased to be an issue the moment I took on this position."

An odd thing to say, Obi-Wan thought, for a man who had developed his own security force, the Red Guard, whose masked members used force pikes as weapons.

"I'll order a lockdown," Palpatine said. "That means every door will open only with a retinal scan."

"Omega and Zan Arbor are probably already in the building," Obi-Wan said. "My guess is that Teda got them past security."

"I have monitors on the water system," Palpatine said. "There are no reports of sabotage."

"I advise you to shut down the entire system," Obi-Wan said. "We can't take a chance."

Palpatine hesitated. Then he got out his comlink, notified Mas Amedda, and gave the order.

"And now I will go to the assembly," he said.

"But Supreme Chancellor, you can't," Obi-Wan argued.

"But Master Kenobi, I must," Palpatine said softly. For the first time in his acquaintance with the Supreme Chancellor, Anakin sensed something underneath his composure — just a hint of anger, striking as fast as a serpent, and then gone.

A red light began to glow on Palpatine's comlink.

"The most serious alert," he murmured, and accessed it. He listened for a moment, then shut it down.

"It could be nothing. A valve in a water tunnel won't function. They wouldn't have noticed it, but when they shut down the water system, the valve came up as nonfunctioning."

"Where?"

Palpatine gave him the coordinates, and Obi-Wan turned to Anakin. "Stay with the Chancellor."

"But Master —"

"Anakin, stay! Don't leave him!" Obi-Wan's order floated back to Anakin as his Master ran off.

CHAPTER SEVENTEEN

Stay.

Obi-Wan was off to face Granta Omega, and Anakin was now just a *bodyguard.*

Palpatine's pale gaze studied him.

"You can go."

"I can't disobey my Master. I can't leave you alone."

"If I call my Red Guard they can be here in three minutes. Less."

"It would not matter," Anakin said miserably. "Obi-Wan told me to stay."

"Well, let us walk, then. I am scheduled to preside over the vote on Senator Divinian's proposal."

"But my Master told you not to go."

"True. But unlike you, I do not have to obey an order of caution."

Caution. Obi-Wan's caution drove Anakin crazy.

"The work of the Senate goes on," Palpatine continued as they began to walk. "To keep going on, no matter what the obstacles — that is what a leader must do. I have learned, Anakin, over the course of my political career, one important thing: I cannot let anyone get in the way of my service. In the beginning, I doubted myself. Who am I, I asked myself, to decide fates, to make rulings? Then the answer came to me. I must do it because there is no one else who can do it better." Palpatine chuckled. "Oh, I'm not saying I'm keeping the Republic together singlehandedly. But fate has thrust me into this position — and I would be untrue to myself as well as the galaxy if I did not utilize everything I have and everything I am in order to succeed at it."

Palpatine's serenity was almost eerie. It was as though, Anakin thought suddenly, Palpatine was *above* this, looking down. As though criminals like Granta Omega were merely toys to be observed. Where did he get that confidence? Anakin was reaching out blindly, trying to probe the Supreme Chancellor, but his powers were not that developed. He kept meeting a wall.

"What I wish," Palpatine said, "is that you will realize this one day, too. That it is right to use every means at your disposal. I'm sure your Master would agree."

Anakin had his doubts. He saw Siri and Ferus pounding down the hallway.

"Ah," Palpatine said. "Reinforcements."

Siri halted in front of them. "Where is Obi-Wan?"

"There was a security breach and he went to check it out," Anakin explained.

"Coordinates," Siri rapped out.

Anakin gave them to her, and she turned to Ferus. "Stay here with the Supreme Chancellor. I'll contact you if you're needed."

Ferus nodded. He did not seem to have the same conflict about the order that Anakin did. Siri raced down the hall.

"You go, too, Anakin," Palpatine urged him. "One Jedi is enough protection."

Anakin hesitated. He would be disobeying a direct order from Obi-Wan. But Obi-Wan had given the order before Ferus had shown up. And even though Palpatine had dismissed the idea that the water valve malfunction could be a security breach, Anakin felt in his bones that it was Omega, just as Obi-Wan had.

"If it is Omega, he is too dangerous an opponent to allow to escape," Palpatine said. "The future of the Senate is at stake."

Ferus said nothing. His dark eyes moved from

Palpatine to Anakin. He knew that whatever he said, Anakin would not take it into consideration.

Anakin made his decision. He turned to Ferus. "I have to go. Don't leave his side."

He didn't have time to wonder if Ferus was annoyed that he had given a fellow Padawan an order. He felt the urgency of his mission. Everything in him pointed the way to a showdown with Omega. And it was just as Palpatine had said: Only he knew what he was capable of. Only he knew the right thing to do.

CHAPTER EIGHTEEN

Obi-Wan splashed through the water tunnel. There were only a few centimeters of water on the bottom, but the tunnel was sweating water, and it dripped steadily on his head and down his neck. He had examined the valve that caused the malfunction alarm, and he was almost certain it had been caused by a blow, probably from a tool. There was a deep, fresh scratch on the valve, and part of the edge of it was bashed in, lying flush against the tunnel itself, making it impossible to open it. Had Omega and Zan Arbor attempted to open the valve and failed? Was the damage a result of frustration, or miscalculation?

It didn't matter. What mattered was that they were here.

The sound of dripping water magnified in his ears

until the soft *plinks* sounded like loud *clangs*. There were so many branches of the tunnel that he wasn't even sure where the main tunnel ran. He wasn't lost, exactly — not yet — but he wasn't terribly comfortable with his sense of direction at this point. Obi-Wan splashed down another quarter-kilometer. He had to go slowly, for fear of making too much noise, but at this rate, he'd never find them. The Senate complex was as large as a mid-sized city on some planets. If Omega and Zan Arbor decided to hide, it could take some time before he could find them.

Obi-Wan's comlink signaled, and he grabbed it. It was Tyro. The reception was poor, and the com line crackled.

"Obi-Wan, I must meet with you. Where are you?"

"In the water tunnels. Tyro, I don't have time —"

"Listen to me. I've dug back, looking for links. And I stumbled on something. Something . . . much more . . . terrible."

Even through the poor connection, Obi-Wan heard the fear in Tyro's voice. "I know about the assassination plot on Palpatine," Obi-Wan told his friend.

"What? No . . ." The comlink crackled again. ". . . can't talk about it over a comlink. We must meet. This involves the highest level . . . great evil . . ."

"I know, Tyro!" Obi-Wan hissed into the comlink, exasperated. "Sano Sauro!"

". . . only you can truly understand . . ." Tyro said through the static.

"Tyro? I can't pick up what you're saying! I'll get back to you as soon as I can." Obi-Wan shut off the transmission. He saw a schematic blueprint on the side of the tunnel, and he hurried over to examine it.

The blueprint was fashioned by raised laser lines that responded to touch. When Obi-Wan touched one part of the blueprint, it lit up in far more detail.

Just like the blueprint at the factory on Falleen.

They had used the same system to map the tunnels. Did that mean that the tunnels in the factory on Falleen corresponded to the Senate tunnels?

Obi-Wan touched the area he was standing in. The tunnel design appeared, with all the different branches.

He didn't recognize the design. It was different from the one on Falleen. But that didn't mean that another quadrant wouldn't match. If he found the quadrant that they'd built on Falleen, he'd know which way Zan Arbor and Omega were going.

Which meant he would have to flash through each quadrant of the Senate water system until he found the one that matched. Obi-Wan scanned the menu. There were five hundred and seventy-two separately designated quadrants to the system. It would take too long for him to stand here and try to match them.

Obi-Wan studied the tunnel around him in frustration. The answer was here. Somewhere. There was something he wasn't seeing.

He closed his eyes, remembering the tunnel on Falleen. Had there been a clue there that he had missed?

In his mind, he saw the tunnel he was standing in and matched it to the one on Falleen. Something was different, he knew. What? Suddenly, he realized something crucial.

Vents.

The Senate water tunnel had no vents. Of course not. It had valves to regulate water flow.

The tunnel on Falleen had vents.

Obi-Wan bent forward and accessed the grid again. He saw on the menu that the air and water tunnels were stacked on top of one another. There were several linking passageways for workers to get from one to the other. He pressed the key for the air tunnel quadrant nearest to where he was standing.

It was the same grid.

Obi-Wan realized then what he should have realized on Falleen. Zan Arbor had attempted to transmit the Zone through water to a large population. She had failed.

TRACK A EXPERIMENT VOIDED.
TRACK B EXPERIMENT BEGUN.

Track A had been transmission through water. It had failed. Four deaths were the result.

Track B had been transmission through air.

Obi-Wan's conclusions thudded through his brain with sickening logic.

Zan Arbor and Omega knew he was expecting them to attack through water.

They had wanted *the Senate water tunnels to be shut down.*

It was their way in. And while the water tunnels were being searched, they would release the Zone into the air.

He studied the blueprint again, then whipped out his comlink as he ran. He could not get through. He was too deep in the system now.

He ran along the tunnel until he saw the light indicating a pass-through to the air tunnels. He accessed the door and rushed through, then jumped on a constantly moving platform that took him up to the air transport systems. Obi-Wan raced through a circular door into the air tunnel.

He remembered the blueprint perfectly. If he took a left turn, then a right, he would arrive in the main air tunnel. The one that went to the main Senate chamber.

He ran down the tunnel, his footsteps making no noise. Before long he heard a faint humming noise.

A speeder bike.

He took the next turn and saw them. Zan Arbor and Omega, traveling at low speed through the tunnel.

He accessed the Force and leaped, throwing himself through the air, straight at the speeder.

CHAPTER NINETEEN

Obi-Wan hit the end of the vehicle and grabbed on to the edge of the backseat. The speeder lurched with the impact and collided with the wall in a shower of sparks.

In the pilot seat, Granta Omega took a backward glance and saw him. A look of rage transfixed his features into a snarling mask.

"Granta, watch out!" Zan Arbor screamed.

The tunnel curved and now the speeder was heading straight for the wall. Omega jerked the controls. The rear fishtailed wildly, tossing Obi-Wan back and forth. He scrambled toward the third seat in the rear.

Zan Arbor took out a blaster. Obi-Wan activated his lightsaber while she lifted it to aim. He swung, deflecting fire, but it was hard to hold on with one hand and he knew he wouldn't be able to do it for long.

"Faster!" she shouted to Omega. With the other hand, she took another blaster out of her belt. "Just drive!"

To his surprise, she did not aim the second blaster at him. Omega piloted the speeder bike closer to the walls of the tunnel, and she took aim at the side.

At the vent.

Obi-Wan realized she wasn't holding an ordinary blaster. It was likely packed with pellets. She was going to shoot into the vent. And right about now, if he remembered the blueprints correctly, they were on a direct line to the main Senate chamber.

"Get closer!" Zan Arbor screamed. She half-stood, half-crouched on the seat, lining up her shot, ignoring Obi-Wan for now. She would only get one chance at the vent.

But Obi-Wan was well aware that Omega had two problems: He had to get close enough for Zan Arbor to shoot, but he had to keep Obi-Wan off balance enough to prevent him from reaching Zan Arbor.

The Force hummed in the tunnel and around him. Time slowed down. Only a second remained until Zan Arbor would take her shot, but that second broke down into smaller pieces of time that Obi-Wan could use.

He could see the vent approaching. He waited until he knew Omega would have to get the speeder closer to the wall. At the moment Omega made the adjustment, Obi-Wan threw himself forward, knocking Zan Arbor off position. With a swift, precise kick, Obi-Wan dislodged the blaster from her hand. It flew out, bouncing against the tunnel wall.

Zan Arbor crouched in the bottom of the speeder, her face contorted in a scream.

"Do it now!" she screamed at Omega.

Of course. Omega would have a blaster, too. He always had a backup.

Omega threw the speeder into reverse. It was careening now, almost out of control, but his arm was steady as he aimed the blaster at the vent.

Again, time moved for Obi-Wan just as he wanted it to move, with spaces in between the seconds for him to exploit. He reached over and pushed the speed lever forward. The speeder went into maximum velocity in resverse.

Obi-Wan was prepared, but Omega and Zan Arbor were thrown forward with the lurch of speed. Omega let go of the blaster. Obi-Wan reached up and snatched it out of the air, then tucked it into his utility belt.

Omega tried to push the engines into forward again, but the speeder finally protested and stalled. The engine cut out and the speeder spun crazily, then bounced on the bottom of the tunnel and slammed against the wall.

Omega was already jumping out as the speeder bike died. Obi-Wan leaped after him, but found himself suddenly contending with a dozen miniature seeker droids hammering blaster fire at him. Omega had released them from a compartment on the speeder even as it came to its final stop.

The first dozen were joined by another dozen. Then another. And, Obi-Wan saw in dismay, another. The blaster fire kept Obi-Wan moving, but he could not get anywhere. He had to leap and defend himself against the blaster fire while taking down the elusive droids, who were now between him and the two criminals.

Zan Arbor ran toward Omega. "Let's move on to the exit plan."

Omega stood, watching Obi-Wan contend with the droids. Obi-Wan heard him clearly. "I want to see him die. Not even a Jedi can escape this many seekers."

"Don't be a fool. Come on! Security will be all over us in another minute!" Zan Arbor started to run.

Taking a last look at Obi-Wan, Omega grinned. "Have fun."

Then he turned and started after Zan Arbor.

Obi-Wan leaped into the air, barely missing blaster

crossfire. The tunnel was filling with smoke from the heavy fire. He began to regret charging off alone to hunt Omega. Maybe he'd been wrong not to wait for backup . . .

Jedi do not second-guess.

Especially when they are in a tunnel with thirty-three flying, firing droids.

Three droids in one blow. But there were thirty others, and it would take time.

Instead of running forward, Obi-Wan retreated. He dashed back to the speeder and threw himself underneath it. His face was directly against the hot metal, his arms and legs squeezed inside so that the blasters could get not direct shots at him.

He heard the blaster fire rake the speeder, front to back, searching for his position. He waited until he heard the distinctive sound of several rounds of blaster fire penetrate the fuel tank.

He had enough time, he had more than enough time, thanks to the Force, but Obi-Wan felt the hair on the back of his neck singe as he flew through the air, escaping the exploding speeder bike. The fireball took out twenty-eight seeker droids at once. Obi-Wan slashed the remaining two as he moved through the air, propelled by the Force and the extremely hot air thrown off by the explosion.

He landed on his feet — singed, but fine.

He started to run, whipping out his comlink as he moved. He knew where they were going. The Senate landing platform.

He tried his comlink, but the heat of the blast had fused it. Obi-Wan tossed it away as he doubled his speed. The landing platform must be ahead. Omega and Zan Arbor had mapped out a plan that would get them inside the air tunnel and then out of the Senate as fast as possible.

Obi-Wan saw an air vent dangling off its hinges. He rushed forward and peered inside. Only a few meters of crawl space separated him from the vast landing platform. He crawled through.

The landing platform was kilometers long, big enough to park space freighters in, though most often it was used for the smaller transports of the Senators and important guests. Vehicles were parked in orderly rows. There was no sign of Omega or Zan Arbor. They were undoubtedly racing toward their transport and he could waste an hour looking for them and never find them. Omega would escape again. He had prevented the Zone from penetrating the Senate, and had stopped the assassination of Palpatine — he hoped. Omega was leaving in defeat.

None of that mattered. Defeat or not, Omega was still escaping.

Obi-Wan gathered the Force around him. He had never needed it more. To his surprise, he felt it move like a gathering storm, already powerful but hinting at the greater strength to come.

Anakin.

His apprentice moved out from an aisle of transports, racing toward him. Siri was by his side.

"Palpatine?" he asked Anakin.

"I left him with Ferus," Anakin replied. "Omega?"

"Here somewhere." Anakin had left Palpatine? He'd given him a direct order! Of course, Ferus must have arrived, and the situation had changed. But he had wanted Anakin to stay with the Chancellor because if he had missed something, Anakin would still have a chance to foil an attack.

"We tracked you through the tunnel," Siri said.

Anakin was turning, his eyes raking the platform. Obi-Wan felt the Force build. He reached out, looking at the platform, searching for the dark Force that was here, concealed, trying to hide.

"There." Anakin pointed. "Third aisle over. Thirty-seven transports down."

They raced down a parallel aisle, hoping to surprise them.

They stealthily moved around a gleaming transport.

Across the aisle, Omega and Zan Arbor were already seated in the cockpit of a sleek space cruiser. Omega was quickly instituting takeoff procedures.

No time for delay or to make a plan. The Jedi charged. Anakin accessed the Force and leaped straight onto the windscreen, startling Zan Arbor, who screamed. Obi-Wan landed on the roof and leaned over. He withdrew his lightsaber, ready to cut a hole in the door panel below. Siri leaped up next to him.

"It really gets tiresome to be continually underestimated."

The voice was Omega's. He was transmitting outside the cockpit.

Grimly, Obi-Wan started to cut.

"Do you really think you have foiled my plans, simply by showing up here? If you cut through that door panel, Obi-Wan, you will kill thousands of Senators."

Obi-Wan continued to cut.

"Obi-Wan," Siri whispered.

"That's right, Master Tachi. This will be a day the Senate will long remember. A bloodbath."

"He has a transmitting device," Anakin said from his position outside the windscreen.

Obi-Wan stopped his effort.

"Ah, better. Let me explain. I have programmed hundreds of seeker droids with the vital information to key Senators as well as to Palpatine. All I have to do is push the button."

Obi-Wan felt rage build up inside him. He could not, would not let Omega blackmail him into letting him escape. But he had no doubt that Omega was telling the truth. It was similar to the way he had orchestrated the death of Jedi Master Yaddle.

He felt the Force move, a boiling mass that caused him and Siri to jump to their feet on top of the cruiser. Anakin was up, hanging in midair for the second it took him to slash through the windscreen directly in front of a shocked Omega. He jumped directly on top of the melted material, material that must have been too hot to stand on. Zan Arbor screamed as the melted windscreen fell into her lap.

Obi-Wan had never seen such speed. Even he could not fully track his apprentice's movement. Balancing on the lip of the cruiser, faster than sight, Anakin reached in and grabbed the transmitter from Omega's clutches.

"Whoops, no more button," he hissed at Omega.

With a cry of rage, Omega triggered the powerful engines. The cruiser shot up so fast all the Jedi slipped off. They fell to the ground as Omega took off in a burst of speed, clipping a cruiser's wing as he went and knocking over a row of swoops and disrupting traffic in the nearest sky lanes.

Obi-Wan watched from the floor, momentarily stunned.

Anakin looked at the transmitter in his hand.

"He lied," he said. "The transmitter is locked in position. He has already programmed the droids."

CHAPTER TWENTY

"The fastest way back to the Senate chamber is though the tunnels," Siri said.

"We don't know the way," Anakin said.

"If I know Ferus, he does," Siri said crisply.

They ran back to the vent and crawled through, then ran down the air tunnel. As she ran, Siri flipped open her comlink and contacted Ferus. Quickly, she filled him in.

"We're just entering the main Senate chamber," Ferus said. "There's no sign of any trouble."

"Stay with Palpatine. Contact Master Windu and request reinforcements. Can you get us through the tunnels to the chamber?"

"Yes. I loaded the Senate utility tunnels onto my datapad."

"Bring us in on a middle tier."

There was a pause of only seconds. "Travel back to the ZM7789 section. Look for vent ZM22899. Go through that one. It will ascend two hundred meters and make a sharp turn to vent UB339. Go through that. Follow that tunnel straight to vent NW993. That comes out into the Senate chamber."

"Got it."

They moved fast, running now. Siri kicked in the first vent. This tunnel was large enough for them to walk in, but as Ferus had told them, it turned sharply upward for two hundred meters. They used their cable launchers to swiftly vault up.

"A sharp turn here." Siri kicked in the next vent.

She ran ahead, and Obi-Wan had a chance to talk to Anakin.

"You left the Supreme Chancellor."

"Ferus was there."

"You could have contacted me."

"There wasn't time."

"And now there are hundreds of seeker droids heading to the Senate and only one Jedi available to protect Chancellor Palpatine and the Senators."

Obi-Wan saw Anakin's mouth tighten. He grew less and less open to correction from his Master. It had

been the opposite for Obi-Wan. The longer they were together, the more he welcomed Qui-Gon's remarks, even
when they were critical.

"I'm at the next vent!" Siri cried. "I can hear something. Hurry!"

They scurried through the next vent, then ran down
the tunnel to the last one, Siri in the lead. Now they
could hear it — blaster fire. Shouts. The random, terrible noise of violent chaos.

They burst out on a mid-level tier of the chamber.
The seeker droids were everywhere, looking for their
targets. Senators marooned in pods dove to the floor.
Bodyguards tried to protect their charges and seeker
droids went after them as well.

"I don't see Palpatine!" Siri yelled. "He's not in his
pod."

"He could be stuck on one of the tiers," Obi-Wan
said.

Siri called Ferus on the comlink but there was no
answer. He was either too busy to answer or his comlink wasn't functioning.

They didn't know where to start, so they started
where they were. Anakin was a flash in the air as he
moved, targeting droids as they dipped and revolved,
spraying blaster fire toward their targets. Obi-Wan saw a
seeker droid homing in on a Senator cowering in his

pod, at least fifty meters below. He jumped off the tier into the pod, taking the droid down in mid-leap.

Siri leaped from pod to pod, slashing at seeker droids in the air as she went and ricocheting blaster bolts back into the droids. Many exploded as their fire was returned to them. With a quick glance Obi-Wan saw them flame out and fall far below to the ground floor. They were hundreds of meters in the air, and the droids had the advantage. They could fly. The Jedi needed an edge.

Obi-Wan leaped down to the next tier and found a terrified assistant hiding among the opulent drapery of the pod from the planet Belazura. It was still tethered to its docking point.

"Show me the main controls for the pods," Obi-Wan said.

"I-I-" the aide stammered, too terrified to speak.

"Do it now!" Obi-Wan barked.

The durasteel in Obi-Wan's voice caused the aide to snap to attention. "There's a control on level 125. . . ."

"Let's go."

Obi-Wan leaped into the pod. He pressed the indicator to bring them down ten levels. The pod dropped like a stone.

The pod docked at Tier 125. "Come on," Obi-Wan said.

The aide darted forward, running low to make himself less of a target. Still, every spray of blaster fire caused him to yelp in fear.

Obi-Wan protected him as they ran. The aide quickly leaped behind a large column. He grimaced when he saw a security officer on the ground, but he moved to a panel in the wall. "Here," he said, accessing the panel. "These controls can override the individual pod controls."

Obi-Wan quickly scanned the controls. He pushed several indicators, watching the pods move on a diagram. By moving large blocs of pods, he created a stepping-stone effect throughout the Senate chamber.

"Stay here, you'll be safer," he told the aide.

With a glance down at the dead guard at his feet, the young aide nodded shakily. "Whatever you say."

Obi-Wan raced back to the tier. He could see that he had been successful. Siri was already jumping from pod to pod, able now to cover more airspace. Anakin was doing the same. When Obi-Wan looked down, he could see, far below, Jedi charging out onto the Senate floor. He saw Shaak Ti leaping onto the pods like steps, moving upward. A team led by Coleman Trebor used the pod controls to move closer to their goal, then leaped into the air to take out two, four, seven, ten seeker droids at once during their descent.

Obi-Wan saw Palpatine at last. He stood on a tier far below, facing out toward the melee. Ferus stood in front of him, angling his lightsaber to fend off blaster bolts fired by the droids. Palpatine hardly noticed the Jedi protecting him. His bleak gaze swept the chamber.

Then Obi-Wan saw Roy Teda on the same tier, making his way forward. A droid was tracking him, Obi-Wan saw, and Teda knew it. He was running for his life.

Omega had betrayed Teda, as he eventually betrayed all who joined forces with him. He had programmed a seeker droid to assassinate Teda, too.

Obi-Wan leaped onto a pod twenty meters down. He knew he was too far to reach the tier in time, but he had to try. As he made his way down, his lightsaber never stopped moving, swiping at the droids who were zeroing in on terrified Senators.

He was close enough now to see the snarl of fury and terror on Teda's face, and suddenly, Obi-Wan guessed his intent. If he was going to go down, he wanted the seeker droid to take down Palpatine, too.

Obi-Wan leaped, then leaped again. Just below, Teda ran. Ferus had turned to deal with a storm of blaster fire from five droids heading his way. Far below Ferus, Siri had seen nothing. Anakin had made his way down to the Senate floor and was on his way back up again. He had landed in a large pod and was in the middle of protecting an entire delegation.

Obi-Wan continued to make his way down, slicing

through droids as he went. The Senate chamber was filled with shouts and screams, the smoke of blasters, and the unmistakable smell of fear.

Teda was only a few steps from Palpatine when Ferus moved. Obi-Wan had never seen him turn, had never seen him notice Teda, yet suddenly, Ferus's arm moved backward. Without even looking, he took out the lead seeker droid that had been targeting Teda.

Then Ferus turned his full attention to the droids. He Force-leaped upward, the bronze glow of his lightsaber a constantly moving presence, arcing and circling, slashing, flipping backward, moving forward.

Even as he leaped down the final meters toward Ferus, Obi-Wan saw the droids fall. Only one remained. Teda drew a blaster to fire at Ferus, but the droid suddenly dipped and fired, and Teda fell, smoke rising from the exit wound in his back. Ferus slashed the droid in half and bent over Teda. Obi-Wan could see by the posture of Ferus's body that it was too late.

Obi-Wan landed at last. "Good work, Ferus."

Ferus's mouth was tight. "I was too late."

Even though Teda was an enemy of the Jedi, Ferus felt he had failed.

Obi-Wan repeated the words he had spoken, this time in a gentle tone. "Good work, Ferus."

Ferus turned to look out over the chamber. "The tide has turned."

The Jedi and security forces were gaining the upper hand. Senators had been herded out of the chamber to safety. Others were being protected. The Jedi teams were now destroying the last of the droids. Obi-Wan glanced quickly over the chamber, searching for a Jedi who might need his help. Suddenly he heard his name being called.

"Obi-Wan!"

It was Tyro. Obi-Wan half-turned, searching for his friend.

Tyro stood in the back of the tier, half-shrouded in darkness. He darted forward toward Obi-Wan, straight into the path of a seeker droid homing in on Palpatine.

"Tyro, drop!" Obi-Wan shouted, already moving.

Ferus leaped as the droid fired. He deflected the fire from Palpatine, but it was too late for Tyro.

Tyro fell on his knees, riddled with blaster fire.

"NO!" The cry was torn from Obi-Wan's chest. *No, no, not Tyro, not him, not this, I cannot bear this. . . .*

He ran toward him, his legs propelling him forward while a part of him deep inside was still with dread, knowing what the next seconds would bring.

Tyro met his eyes. There was infinite sadness in his

gaze, infinite regret. He opened his mouth but could not speak.

Tyro lifted his hand. It trembled as he opened his palm toward Obi-Wan. He closed his hand into a fist and placed it against his heart.

Then he looked beyond Obi-Wan's shoulder, behind him. Fear flickered in his eyes. And then he was gone.

Obi-Wan bent over him. He opened his own hand. He closed it. He placed it against Tyro's chest and bowed his head over his beloved friend. He murmured the words every Svivreni told a loved one before a journey.

"The journey begins," Obi-Wan whispered. "So go."

CHAPTER TWENTY-ONE

The next day, the vote was finally held. There was no debate. Senator Bog Divinian's proposal to bar the Jedi from any action taken on behalf of the Senate was soundly defeated. Even Sano Sauro voted against it. It was noted that the two of them had arrived well after the previous day's events.

Bog was disgraced. Back on his planet, those who had once been his supporters demanded his resignation. Everyone but Bog knew his political career was over.

Because of his coolness on the day of the attempted massacre, Supreme Chancellor Palpatine's stature increased, and he was more powerful than ever. Twenty-one Senators died that day, fourteen aides, and ten

Senatorial guards. It was considered a miracle that the numbers weren't higher.

For a day or two, the Senators seemed bound in a common grief. But after the memorials and the speeches were over, the blame began. Who had allowed it to happen? What committee had not forseen it? What faction had secretly approved of it? Who had not condemned it loudly enough?

Charges and countercharges. Speeches. Lectures. Tirades.

Obi-Wan was sick of it. Sick at heart.

He sat in Tyro's cluttered office. He had attended Tyro's memorial service, which was packed with friends, with more spilling out into the hallways, unable to participate or hear, but still wanting, needing to be present. Obi-Wan had no idea that so many had loved him.

But here, among his beloved files and documents, here was where Obi-Wan felt closest to him.

He had thought he couldn't bear this death. But of course he had.

There would be more to bear, he knew. The growing darkness that Master Windu had spoken of was now in his heart. He could feel that darkness with every breath he took.

He had searched through Tyro's files, through his datapad, through everything he could think of. There was no record of what Tyro had been trying to tell him. Obi-Wan could not make sense of it.

I stumbled on something. Something . . . terrible.

. . . the highest level . . . great evil . . .

. . . only you can truly understand . . .

What was it? Obi-Wan silently asked Tyro. *What were you going to tell me?*

He had assumed that the seeker droid that killed Tyro was heading for Palpatine. Yet the Senate investigator had told him that morning that it was programmed to hit Tyro.

Why would Omega want to kill a lowly Senate aide? It didn't make sense.

He might never know the answer.

Obi-Wan looked around at the tiny office. He had arranged for Tyro's files to be moved to the Temple, where a team under the supervision of Madame Jocasta Nu would go over everything. There could have been something Obi-Wan missed.

By tonight, the office would be cleared. Knowing the demand for Senate space, by tomorrow, the office would already be occupied. Any memory of Tyro would be swept out with the dust.

Reluctant to leave, Obi-Wan lingered. He heard soft footsteps outside in the hallway, and Astri appeared in the doorway.

"They said I could find you here," she said. "I'm sorry about your friend."

Obi-Wan nodded his thanks. "And how are you?"

"I am good," she said softly. "So are Lune and Didi. Thanks to you. Bog has been stripped of power, and he is now useless to the Commerce Guild and Sano Sauro. That means he is powerless to hurt us, too."

"So what will you do?"

She shrugged. "I'm not sure. Didi wants to return to Coruscant, but I don't know." She hugged herself and shivered. "It has changed. I don't like it here anymore. I'm fearful here, but I don't know of what."

"I know what you mean," Obi-Wan murmured. He rose and came toward her. He raised a hand and switched off the lights in Tyro's office, feeling something break inside him as he did so. Tyro was gone forever.

They walked down the hallway together.

"My advice," Obi-Wan said, "is to pick a pleasant world with a genuinely democratic government. Raise your son." He smiled. "Keep Didi out of trouble. And always remember I am here for you," Obi-Wan said.

"As you have proven time and time again," Astri said.

She stopped and put two hands on his shoulders. Her dark eyes searched his.

"I see the sorrow in you," she said. "I can't take it

away. But you have saved me and those that I love. Know that, at least."

The small moments, Obi-Wan thought, as he laid a hand over Astri's. They did not measure up against the times of sorrow. But they had to be enough.

Anakin sat with Palpatine inside the Chancellor's office. They looked out together at the temporary garden planted in an exterior courtyard of the Senate complex. Below, Anakin saw the tops of trees, delicate green leaves against silver bark. Running in a square outside the trees was the colorful splash of exotic flowers. Towering above the flowers were twin horns of the bloodred *claing* bush, native to Sano Sauro's world.

"I don't understand," he said to Palpatine. "You gave Senator Sauro the position of Deputy Chancellor. We are certain that he was in on the plot to assassinate you."

"I offered it before the vote on the Jedi petition, knowing he could not refuse," Palpatine said. "I knew he would betray Bog. The assurance of a powerful office would be enough to abandon a risky scheme."

"But you rewarded Sauro for betraying you."

"I have made my enemy my friend," Palpatine said. "His fate is now linked with mine. And I will always know what he's up to."

Anakin nodded. He would miss these talks with Palpatine. He felt that he was learning, even though he had not yet been able to sift through the nuggets of wisdom.

"I have asked you here to thank you for your efforts on that day," Palpatine said. "The Senate came close to being destroyed. Please do not fault me for saying this, but I feel that your Jedi Council did not fully appreciate what you did that day. I watched you. I saw how many you saved. I understand that Ferus Olin was given a special commendation for what he did. I don't understand."

"You don't? He saved your life."

Palpatine stared out at the vast Coruscant cityscape. "Good of him, of course. But no more than he was asked to do. Whereas you, Anakin, always do more. I just think it's a pity that the Council doesn't see that. Perhaps I should talk to Master Yoda —"

"No," Anakin said quickly. "He would think I wanted you to speak to him about me, that I was seeking approval. Jedi do not seek approval."

"Then tell me, Anakin. From the point of view of a Jedi, since it is sometimes difficult for those of us outside your order to understand it. Why did Ferus Olin receive special notice, and you did not?"

"Because he did his duty," Anakin said. He tasted

bitterness in his mouth. "He obeyed his Master and stayed at his post. He saved your life and dozens of other lives."

"You saved more."

"It was not a contest."

"No. It was a battle." Chancellor Palpatine sighed. He looked back at the garden.

Through the transparent screen that separated them, Anakin saw Obi-Wan enter Palpatine's office. His Master saw them outside. He waited, not wanting to interrupt.

"I see your Master has arrived to fetch you," Palpatine said, rising. "I want you to feel free to visit me from time to time, Anakin. I know you have other missions. And I know you will perform splendidly. I for one am glad you are on my side."

"I am honored," Anakin said. He bowed his goodbye.

"Granta Omega," Obi-Wan said once Anakin had joined him in the hall. "We don't know where he is. But we know where he's been."

Anakin looked back at Palpatine. Studying the Senate had not been as bad as he'd thought. He'd been close to great power, the greatest in the galaxy, and he felt he was just on the verge of learning more about it.

But he felt he was not meant for power struggles

and intrigue — not yet. He did not like to think about why the Jedi Council was so hard on him, about why Ferus earned recognition from the Council when he did not.

He did not want these feelings. He wanted them to fall away and leave him with his core, a core that was not threatened by what other beings thought or said. On a mission, everything else did fall away. He was able to concentrate, to focus.

He turned back to his Master. He was ready to go.